Pandəmonium Tales

Godiva Glenn

Lunar Mischief Press, L.L.C.

PANDƎMONIUM TALES

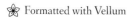 Formatted with Vellum

Demon Of Her Dreams

Chapter 1

Moisture pressed to the side of her neck as he kissed her there and drew his tongue across her skin, tasting her. Farrah shivered, and a scream welled inside her, but didn't escape. She could try to scream and yell, but nothing ever came out. Whenever he appeared, it wasn't her dream anymore. She couldn't control it.

Tonight.

The word made her cold. He didn't speak, exactly; the hissing sound of his voice broadcasted directly into her brain. The nightmare never made sense, yet his single word held confidence. It was a promise, one she didn't want him to succeed in keeping.

Submit.

That word was a constant. Every chase, every night, all came down to his insistence that she submit. She never would.

He buried his face into the black, curly mass of her hair and inhaled so deeply she could hear it. When he exhaled, it tickled her scalp. He caressed her sides with his long, black claws and kissed her neck again. Her body awakened for a moment, but she shut it down. She knew nothing good could come of giving in to a demon.

Perhaps most of the world would think dreams were just dreams, but Farrah knew better. There were dreams, and then there was this—something dark and complex, and infinitely worse than any bad dream could be. Somehow this nightmare could leech into her reality. She'd started waking up with bruises from where she'd fallen in her dream. That very morning, she'd found scratches over her legs and arms from the heap of rocks she'd spent the night hiding in. Who knew what would happen to her if she gave him what he wanted?

Meanwhile, his touch grew bolder. He inflicted feather-light caresses upon her breasts while he licked up her neck to nibble her ear. She stared forward, her eyes wide open. If she closed them, she knew her body would take it as a sign of welcoming this pleasure. If she stared into the darkness that flickered with shapes and shadows, she could try to think of other things. Things that had nothing to do with the demon holding her.

He squeezed her breast, the tips of his claws digging in through her shirt, not tearing fabric or breaking skin, but just enough to indent her flesh and make her wince.

Submit.

She didn't bother with a reply. Over and over, she'd tried to communicate with the demon. He wouldn't converse, only say the same words, one at a time, more furiously the longer the night stretched. There was no reasoning with a monster.

A low growl vibrated through him, filled with impatience.

Tonight.

Her teeth gritted at the arrogance in his tone. His voice echoed with frustrating confidence in her mind.

Yet she felt it too. Something was different about tonight. How she didn't even recall falling asleep. How soon the darkness had come. How quickly he'd trapped her. She didn't understand how he'd caught her. Usually they were locked in an endless chase, but tonight he seemed to have more power over her dream.

The landscape blurred and changed. The hotel room returned, encased in near pitch-black darkness. The demon pushed her into the center of the room. Farrah looked around in desperation for an escape, but even though this was a replica of her hotel room, the doors were missing. The furniture was decaying as if centuries had passed. Light glowed along seams in the illusion, highlighting the corners of the room, the area beneath the couch where it sat on the floor, and the fractures along the walls—just enough illumination to show the demon's features as he stood before her.

His appearance was already burned into her memory, but still gave her a moment of shock. Tall horns curved away from his forehead, adding to his already impressive height. He was bulky and muscular, and his skin was the mottled color of hot coals, sooty gray and black with faintly glowing veins of red as if lava flowed in his veins.

The crimson vessels stretched over his strong thighs and snaked around the thick column of his cock. She hated that she'd noticed, but there was no avoiding the sight of it. The first night she'd seen him, she'd known exactly what he wanted. A demon wouldn't have that for no reason.

Heat flooded her body and smoke filled her nostrils as her clothing singed away completely. Her hands flew to cover her sudden nakedness. She turned away and hesitated, again realizing there was nowhere to run.

Something wrapped around Farrah's left ankle, then her right. She glanced down to see the ground twisting and writhing to hold her captive. She yanked at her legs until her muscles hurt, but she couldn't break free. Struggling made her fall forward, and she landed hard on her hands and knees.

Lovely.

Chapter 2

The demon was on Farrah in the next instant, pressing his nude form against her back. He nestled his thick cock between her thighs, hot and throbbing, but didn't enter.

She clenched her eyes shut against the sensation of him and everything it did to her body. Though she was as terrified as she always was, a part of her—a teeny, tiny sliver—responded with something other than fear.

He planted his hands on either side of her and shoved his hips forward, grinding his hard length along her folds. He slid against her again and again, rubbing the ridged texture of his cock against her pussy and igniting her sensitive clit. At first there was friction, but it didn't last. Soon her slick arousal spread over him, and he used it to slide up and down her channel, her pussy lips spreading easily.

Farrah's cheeks heated with embarrassment. This was better than fearing for her life, but it shocked her how easily her fear had allowed pleasure to sink in. She had to fight not to writhe against him, had to hold her breath not to moan. She liked it rough, and she'd been alone for far too long. Her body reacted based on memories and long-ignored cravings.

His cock wasn't smooth like a man's. It was rough. Coarse, raised bumps along his length tormented her, the sensation blurring her thoughts and rationale. His dominating and possessive nature called to something within her, a whisper of longing that welcomed his crudeness and the way he took what he wanted.

The demon curled his body over hers and dug one clawed hand into the dusty ground beside her shoulder to steady himself. Soot filled her nostrils and choked her, but the discomfort was negligible when compared to the churning sensations of wicked pleasure within her. He reached his other hand around to grasp her breast, massaging it eagerly. His claws dug at the full flesh of her breast in a way that excited her. The danger made her lightheaded, yet she felt oddly safe within the cage of his limbs.

Her eyes fluttered, the last remnants of her common sense screaming at her. What was she doing? Was she really going to give in now? The hand around her breast twisted her nipple until she gasped, and then it slid down her stomach and between her thighs. The demon spread his fingers on either side of her pussy, pressing the head of his cock against her entrance.

All logic fled her. She held her breath and waited.

He pushed in, and he was so large as to make Farrah squirm and grunt. After only a few seconds, it felt like too much, the pressure and stretch an aching burn even though she was wet and ready. She whimpered and cursed, but he continued to sink in without hesitation.

After a few more agonizing minutes, he withdrew an inch—she sucked in a breath—and then he shot his hips forward, thrusting back in deeper and rougher. Her breath shook free in a sharp cry and she sank to her elbows. Something seemed to trigger in the demon and he snarled at her back. He plunged in farther, and quicker, becoming more bestial and aggressive with each thrust.

She arched her back and her torso bowed, pressing her bare breasts to the ground. Though gritty, it was cool, and the chill contrasted perfectly with the heat of the demon's body curled over her and in her. Her breathing grew shallow. The pain had gone, now a distant soreness. Pleasure had replaced it, an alluring, demanding tide that bubbled deep within her. He felt like nothing she'd ever known or could imagine. He was harder than any man—thicker and hotter too. His cock grazed every inch of her inner walls, burnishing her with the rough mold of his shaft. She felt each of his raised ridges, and with each second, grew dizzier from the overwhelming sensation.

His hand returned to her breast just as he slammed so deep his sac collided with her sensitive mound. His previous thrusts had kissed and bruised her cervix, and this last blow was like a battering ram to her insides. Black spots danced across her already dark and blurry vision. Then he rammed in again, and the shock sent goosebumps over her entire body. Her nipples ached. Her toes curled. The beginning of tears caught on her lashes. She screamed in pain or pleasure; it was impossible to separate the two.

She didn't understand what was happening. She didn't understand why it felt so damn good. She was being forcefully fucked—no, used—by a demon, and she couldn't think straight.

"No more," she pleaded.

He grabbed her shoulder with one hand and snatched a tangle of hair in the other, curving her back further, forcing her into an uncomfortable, nearly painful position. Her breath came in gasps as he held her there, thrusting harder, the power behind each stroke shaking her body and making her breasts bounce as moans staggered from her throat. He pulled on her shoulder to aid in pushing deeper into her, as if he'd impale her—as if he couldn't get far enough inside her to fuck her properly. It hurt, but the ache thrilled her.

Pleasure built low in her belly, a confusing frenzy of sensations fed not only by his cock striking deep inside her, but by the way he tugged sharply on her hair and the danger and excitement of being ravaged by a monster. Her nerves drew taut, and she held her breath until the dam broke and she froze, unable to move while pleasure flooded her senses. Her muscles gave out, and she felt dizzy and limp as her body continued to sway and shake to his actions. Her orgasm shot through her in sporadic bursts, leaving parts of her numb and tingling and over-stimulated. For a moment her body seemed to accommodate him with ease, but as the euphoria of her climax faded, his bruising thrusts became agonizing to her lust-swollen folds.

"Too much," she whimpered, struggling in his hold.

He growled in response, or at least she thought it was a response, until he struck deep and held himself there. Her inner walls trembled, clenching and seeking relief, and then his cock spasmed and filled her with heat. She felt each powerful twitch of his shaft as it surged, sending his seed flooding into her depths. The strange sensation sent another fluttering orgasm through her, making her writhe. This made him grasp her tighter, his claws digging into her shoulder as he held her still and emptied his cock.

His entire body vibrated as he finished and stilled, and Farrah slumped forward as he released her. She collapsed, spread out on the cool ground, exhausted and dazed. The motion pulled him free of her, and then the fullness she'd become used to vanished, replaced by the wet sensation of cum dripping down her thighs.

Chapter 3

Farrah closed her eyes and tried to catch her breath, sucking in air as if she'd been saved from drowning. It was over. She would wake now, wouldn't she? But even then, she'd feel forever changed by the encounter. It felt like she'd surrendered something to him, something unspoken and complicated.

After wiping her face with shaking hands, she looked back across her sweat-dampened shoulder and saw him. He was sitting back on his haunches and staring at her. The darkness obscured his face so that she couldn't see his eyes, but it still felt as if she were being scrutinized.

The tightness around her ankles slipped away, and she rolled to her side. The urge to run returned, thrumming in her veins weakly, but consistently. A strange calm descended. The atmosphere changed. The shock and trembling in her body resolved, and she managed to sit up. She scooted away from him with every intent of escaping.

Farrah.

He'd never said her name before, and hearing it now made her breath catch. He reached one hand out. The darkness flickered, and for a moment, his claws vanished to reveal a very human hand, fingertips outstretched toward her. Yet within a blink, his claws returned. He sometimes distorted this way, and she was never sure if it was her imagination or not. It was a nightmare, after all. The concept of real versus imagined was stretched thin and folded over itself.

He cocked his head, long horns catching the flickers of light beyond him in a terrifying silhouette. She shivered, and once again, everything within her vision flashed with light to paint a different scene. For a moment his horns disappeared, and a piercing blue light shone from where his eyes would be, were he not cloaked in shadows.

He crawled toward her, and she watched, entranced. His appearance changed within blinks, back and forth like a strobe light between demon and something else. Something more human. Something vaguely familiar.

When he reached her, however, he was fully a demon again, and a deep growl shook from him. Her surroundings changed again as well, no longer a shadowed version of her hotel room, but the hellish landscape she'd seen before. She still rested against a surface, but it was now a bright mirror. She looked down and saw her own frightened expression staring back. Then she saw him looming over her. The mirror gave light to him, and now his eyes were visible—hard and glossy black. He gripped her left foot and yanked, sliding her back to him, so that she was between his squatting thighs.

Her gaze snared on the thick swell of his cock. She could see it fully now, and her first thought was to marvel at how he'd ever managed to shove it all inside her. Seeing it made her ache. Her pussy clenched at the memory of what they'd just done. It glistened with their mingled fluids, the very sight making her stomach quiver. She felt empty now, and hated how much she wanted to not be empty.

Looking up, she knew he'd caught her staring. A smile curved on his lips before he chuckled, baring gleaming, sharp teeth. The sight and sound unsettled her, and she yanked at her foot in his grasp.

Stay.

Chapter 4

tay.

The command came with a jolt of force that momentarily locked her muscles in place. That he could affect her that way scared her, but she didn't resist. She watched him as he rose, one hand on his cock. Eyes locked on her, he stroked its massive length, growing harder. One glance up at his face and she knew what he wanted. Whether it was a hidden mental command or her own depraved desires, she wasn't certain, but she rose to her knees.

She swallowed as she got a closer look at him, her hand lifting to touch him of its own accord. His shaft was wide and eager, the skin stretched over the straining muscle beneath. She gripped him with a surge of daring. The ridges along his cock throbbed and hardened against her palm. She dragged a fingertip over one and it reacted, transforming from a rigid bump to a nearly sharp barb. They'd felt amazing inside her, and she blushed as she admitted it to herself.

Then Farrah brought her second hand to him. If she wrapped them both around his shaft, her fingertips touched and overlapped to the first section of each joint. He was huge, and holding him like this made her body stir. She became warm, yet uneasy about how she could practically feel her body gushing with slick arousal. That part of her anticipated more. The desire to escape lingered, but it was not nearly so strong.

Sliding her grip up, she brushed the flared collar of his cock's head. It pulsed and swelled with desire. The demon snarled, and the sound was clearly one of satisfaction, not displeasure. Moisture wept from the dark slit centered on his tip. She couldn't resist. She bent forward and probed the slit with her tongue, collecting the fluid there.

He was bitter and spicy, and somehow exactly how she'd imagined a demon might taste. It was strangely intoxicating in a way that made no sense, but Farrah didn't bother overthinking it. Instead she licked around the head of his cock, tasting the remnants of their sex. It was dirty and depraved, and it made her hunger for more.

The pull of her hair gave her pause as the demon reached into the dark curls and held them the way men liked to hold women during oral sex. The sort of grip that was half "let me hold your hair for you," and half "I'm going to hold your head while I fuck your mouth." In this case, however, the insistent scrape of his claws against her scalp let her know that if she wasn't careful, he'd likely fuck her throat with the same fervor he'd used to bruise her insides.

The imagined threat sent a renewed flow of excitement through her, threaded with fear. He likely saw her as holes to be used. It wouldn't be farfetched to assume he wouldn't let her go until she was sore everywhere. That realization didn't worry her, but it should have.

An impatient tug made her redirect her focus. She stroked up and down along his shaft, fascinated by the way it responded, its texture changing as his arousal grew. Pressure on her scalp forced his cockhead between her lips, and she sucked and licked to keep up with the slowly increasing tempo of his rocking hips. She barely had room to swallow, and soon her saliva dripped down his length, aiding her deliberate tugs on his cock.

He forced himself deeper and deeper, until Farrah planted one hand firmly on his length to keep him at bay. His frustration broke through with a growl that vibrated through his entire body and sent a chill down her spine. She closed her eyes as he plunged his cock deeper, breaking her grip on his shaft, until he hit the back of her throat, making her gag and flinch. He dug his claws into her scalp, scratching and twitching. He ignored her struggling and drove in and out of her mouth, fucking her throat and gaining no depth, but leaving her unable to breathe or even think. Tears burned in her eyes from the discomfort and the desperation to suck in air. She no longer gagged, but choked and suffocated. She dug her own nails into his thighs, but his skin was like leather. She couldn't scratch him. He gave no indication of acknowledging her struggle, except that she suspected it made his cock even harder and more unrelenting.

Her pulse thudded in her ears, deafening. The world swam out of focus, and she closed her eyes.

Farrah came to and coughed as the demon slid his dick free of her throat. It took her a moment to stop coughing, and then to realize that she'd lost consciousness. It was probably only for a few seconds, but long enough to douse her hot arousal in the chill of reality.

She clutched her throat and stared up at him. Darkness swathed his face, but she sensed smugness and pride pouring from him. She looked away and pinched her arms. It never worked to wake her, but she still tried. She wouldn't survive this much longer. She trembled from head to toe, lightheaded and exhausted. She needed to wake.

17

Farrah groaned as she tried to stand and crumpled back down to her knees. The demon laughed. The sound echoed in her head, taunting her.

So close. Submit.

She glared at him. "Fuck you."

Chapter 5

N*o. I'll fuck you.*

She froze at his reply, which was the closest they'd ever come to a conversation.

I'll fuck you until you submit. And then I'll fuck you harder. More. Forever.

Bracing herself against the threat, she forced herself to ask, "You can talk now?"

Now that I'm sated enough to think straight.

"And that means—"

Enough talk.

He stepped forward, his erection jutting out. It visibly throbbed, and she stared. The darkness flickered, and within it, the demon's moan slithered through her. When she could see again, she didn't understand what lay before her. His cock had doubled, not in size, but in number. Another appendage sat above the other, as if cloned.

Farrah's jaw dropped and her heart jumped in her chest, ready to beat through her ribcage with terror. She turned, but couldn't move an inch farther before he hauled her back against his body. She struggled, arms swinging and legs kicking with renewed vigor, but he wrestled her down. With one hand, he trapped her wrists high above her head, suspending her over his lap. Her bent legs rested on his muscular thighs. The head of one cock slid against her rear entrance.

"No, no, no," she pleaded, the words falling from her lips with shaky breaths. "Not two."

It has to be two.

"Why? Why is any of this—"

We both want to fuck you. We both need to breed you. The voice paused, and she could hear the smirk lacing his words. We won't go there tonight. Tonight, we breed. That means...

He trailed off, vanishing from her mind. Then he lowered her, and his cocks slid in the lingering wetness of her earlier arousal, but with no insistence. He caressed the front of her body, tweaking her nipples and sighing in pleasure as he did so. Eventually, his touch made it between her thighs. He shoved two clawed fingers into her heat, making her flinch and freeze at the same time. Though they slipped into her easily, she held her breath in fear of the damage the sharp edges could cause. She felt only the slight thickness of them, however, working in and out. He separated his fingers within her, as if testing her or stretching her. She realized what he meant to do, but she couldn't think of it—she refused to. Any moment now, she'd wake up.

Her hips had their own motivation, though. They rocked and rode his fingers, and she bit her lower lip to keep from making a sound of anticipation. She bit until she bled.

Then his fingers were gone, and he reached between their bodies to grip both cocks. He brought them to her entrance and prodded. She almost wanted to laugh at the ridiculousness of it. It wouldn't work. He couldn't... She couldn't...

He pistoned upward, and the stinging sensation of being stretched wide had her gasping and cold. He released her arms and she fell farther onto his cocks, unsupported by his strength. She couldn't think through the pain, only cry out with each breath as she tried, but failed to lift her body from his. He held her hips and forced his way deeper, invading and crowding her pussy.

At first, everything was too tight. She could feel his struggle, and she gritted her teeth as he tried to move in and out, only to seem stuck. He curled over her writhing body and sank his teeth into the slope of her neck. The new sensation helped distract her. He grabbed her breast again and fondled it roughly. It took her a moment to realize he meant to give her some pleasure in the hopes that it would relax her. But there was no relaxing; her muscles had seized around him, yet still he sought to cram himself into her.

While he rolled her nipple between two fingers, he used his free hand to grasp one of hers. He led it between her thighs and forcefully rubbed her hand over her pussy. He couldn't rub her clit himself, she realized—not with those claws. She didn't want to aid him, yet she wanted the pain to subside.

Farrah closed her eyes and slid her fingertips up and down her folds to collect her slick arousal before drawing them to her clit. She bit her tongue and concentrated on that, and on his hands, both of which now massaged her breasts.

It occurred to her that if he were truly a monster, he wouldn't bother softening her up. Surely a demon cared nothing about tearing into her flesh to gain his pleasure. What did it mean that he'd rather coax her to relax?

The thought gave her pause, but only briefly, as his caresses sank through her defenses. The heat of their bodies flowed like a blanket over her, soothing her. Her inner walls relaxed as her pleasure grew, and he drove in deeper, but the pain was a distant ache now.

She leaned back against him as he flicked his tongue over

21

her neck. His rumble was pleasant and satisfied, and she matched it with a soft moan.

Soon he was thrusting deep and hard, each cock pulsating within Farrah and jolting her senses. She felt full to bursting, and when the twin tips reached her end, her walls spasmed and sent an instant, overwhelming climax through her. She rode the waves of euphoria as he fucked her, his intensity increasing until she heard the wet sounds of flesh slapping flesh.

She came down from her bliss, only to be met with an insatiable desire for more. She placed her hands over his where he touched her breasts, and he understood her intention, removing his hands to allow her to touch herself. Instead he clutched her waist and pistoned himself up and up, until his every stroke slammed into the end of her channel.

The sensation was a chaotic blend that left Farrah lightheaded and delirious, as if she were stuck on a continuous orgasm. Her body cramped and convulsed against his plundering cocks, and she welcomed them still. As it went on, her head rolled back against him and she ceased to think or care about anything but the pleasure. She could feel him cresting too, feel the muscles of his arms tighten, his torso flexing against her back. She nearly begged for him to finish, not because she wanted it to end, but because she wanted to feel his climax. One of his hands came up and wrapped around her throat, not cutting off her air completely, but enough that the tension heightened her pleasure.

Holding her there, he froze at the height of a devastating thrust. His cocks pulsed and throbbed, and he groaned above her ear. His chest heaved as he panted. Farrah had no energy to react except to lean harder against him, barely able to keep herself upright.

Then he relaxed his grip, and they sat together in silence as the world continued to flicker with distant lights and moving shadows. He lifted her from his lap and lay her on the ground on her back. Farrah simply breathed and kept her eyes closed, recovering, as she heard and felt him moving around her. She didn't stir until he lifted her again.

Smooth skin rubbed against hers, startling her. Stranger still was the way he touched her with care and gentleness. She was cradled against a pale, warm chest, and she was almost afraid to look up and see the demon's new face. She had a suspicion. Her breathing quickened, and the scent of peppery cologne lingered in the air—a scent she knew too well.

Chapter 6

With his thumb, he stroked Farrah's cheek. "I'm so sorry," he murmured. "I could barely…"

The voice struck her. She dared herself to look up, and there he was, no longer the demon, but her lover. The shock of seeing him now left her speechless for a moment. Her thoughts conflicted, and she had trouble pulling anything together over the steady flow of heat and pleasure from his touch. It was like rising above quicksand, but she eventually did it.

"Nathan," she rasped.

He nodded.

Tears filled her vision, blurring her vision of him—her fiancé, Nathan, killed a year ago this month, just weeks before their wedding.

"Is this a trick?" She shook her head. "Please don't play games with me."

"No game." He bent down and kissed her. His kiss was gentle and familiar, and heartbreaking. Their tongues entwined, and he tasted like he always had, sweet and masculine. It was as if no time had passed. As if he'd never died and left her.

"How?" she asked when he pulled away. She cupped his smooth, warm jaw, a part of her not believing that what she touched was real.

"You wished for me. Over and over." He looked around them where the hellscape continued to flicker. "It reached me when your grief was winning out."

"I don't understand."

"I don't entirely understand it myself. But he does—the other part of me. The part I found while trapped here. Something about you, about us, has opened some sort of way out for me."

She studied his face. He looked exactly like he had the last time she'd seen him. His blue eyes sparkled, even in the darkness. His black hair fell over his forehead in its usual carefree manner. She kept waiting for the darkness to move over him and change him.

"You're not making any sense," she said. "Not that any of this makes any sense."

"I love you."

"I love you too," she whispered, her voice failing her.

"Can you forgive me? For what we—for what I did?"

The joy of holding him, kissing him, of seeing him up close after all this time, made Farrah momentarily forget the rest of the night. The nightmares and the chasing. The pain and the rough coupling. The unexplainable yearning in her response, and the way that somehow, even though it made no sense, she had felt cherished.

"You're the demon," Farrah said.

"He's a part of me, born of what it took to survive the torment here in Pandemonium." His expression grew distant, and a chill invaded his voice. "Though survival is relative. You're dreaming, so you don't see everything that I see. Everything that's here, ready to rip and tear and destroy."

"I don't understand," she confessed. "I know I said that, but this is too much."

He shook his head and softened his tone. "I can explain it all with time. But you have to decide right now, before it's too late. When you wake, I can be with you." He kissed her forehead. "I can return to you."

"What?" Her mind raced, disbelief swept beneath a torrent of joy.

"During the day, I'll be Nathan. But each night, the demon has to return." He looked down at her naked body, but instead of heat in his gaze, there was conflict. "And he'll want you. Sharing your body with him is all I can do to tame him."

"But it's you," she whispered.

"Yes." His face twisted with regret. "I don't want to hurt you, he just... We know your limitations. It's still a dream..."

She stroked her thumb across his cheek, memories assailing her. Her love for him hadn't changed. Her desire to have him hadn't waned. Damn it, she'd missed him. Now she was holding him, and she had a chance to keep him.

"It's real, though," she told him. "Something about these dreams follows me back."

"This world is real, but we can't do actual damage to you." Nathan frowned and exhaled, nuzzling her open palm. "We're connected now. We share the pain and the pleasure, and I want to tell you more, but I'm afraid you'll wake up soon..."

At last, she could have him back with her; that was all she heard. That was all that mattered.

"Yes!" she exclaimed. "Yes!"

Nathan searched her face before giving a slight nod. "Then lie back, love. I'm not done with you. Neither is he. We'll make the most of this dream, and when you wake, we'll make the most of our future."

Demon By Night

Chapter 1

Alyssa peered around the corner. She rarely hid among the reference stacks in the library, and the most recent occurrence was right before she'd thrown caution to the wind and asked Drastos Blake—the mysterious, charming, incredibly sexy research librarian at her university—out to dinner. It seemed fitting that he was once again the reason for her anxiousness and hiding.

They'd had a wonderful date. They'd connected easily with never a dull moment. He'd kissed her goodnight and melted her kneecaps. Then, he'd never called. A week passed and each time she visited him at his desk, it was as if nothing ever happened between them.

She'd known him for four years and been in love with him— or as "in love" as a one-sided situation could go—for three. Asking him to dinner had taken every ounce of her courage, and she was ready to muster up said courage again to now ask, "What the hell?"

Pushing back her shoulders, she inhaled and pictured herself breathing in pure confidence. It was the absolute longest six foot walk of her existence, and the feel of her loose curls bouncing off her shoulders made her feel more comical than serious.

Drastos looked up at her and smiled as he always did, with a mirth that reached his dark eyes and made them seem lighter and full of life. His eyes weren't brown, exactly. More like mahogany. A definite red undertone lurked in their depths and— she ground her teeth. She had a purpose today, and it wasn't to fawn over his eyes.

"You never called," she blurted out. She'd planned to be cool and casual, but her mouth had spoken, so she stood behind it and held his gaze.

His smile slipped for a moment. "I don't think it best to discuss personal matters while I'm working."

"Then when? Could we meet for lunch today?" she asked, not backing down.

His brow furrowed briefly, and he shook his head. "I've already had lunch. Perhaps—" he pursed his lips before continuing. "I think we should just move forward, Ms. Harris."

The use of her last name struck a hard blow. She hadn't been Ms. Harris to him for at least two years. What happened to their first-name basis? She backed away, but before she turned to leave, saw what looked like regret in his eyes.

You're imagining things.

THERE WAS A LINE BETWEEN PERSISTENCE AND STALKING ALYSSA knew this, and she pondered it while waiting beside the steps of the library's main entrance. She hadn't imagined how well their date had gone, nor had she imagined their years' of low-key flirting. How many after-hours university events had they met up at and chatted away into the late night? How many times had he called her over to his desk with extra materials he'd found in his personal time to help with her research?

They had something. Chemistry. Yearning. She wasn't imagining the connection; she was sure of it. All she wanted was the truth from him. She could handle if he told her he didn't feel a spark, but she needed to hear it in plain terms.

When he exited the library, she took a moment to appreciate him in the afternoon light. He was tall, dark, and classically handsome, but the crowning glory of his appearance was in the gentle swoop of silver above his left temple. He wasn't all that much older than Alyssa, and once mentioned he'd had that patch of gray his entire adult life. It was chef's-kiss perfect on him.

His clothing also stood out, being a man who always dressed impeccably, who wore a suit jacket year-round, and never jeans or sneakers. Suits, ties, the occasional waistcoat, and fancy leather shoes — which she bet cost more than one would expect on a librarian's salary — comprised his wardrobe. He had an old-world appearance, which fit him because he was the type to make women swoon.

She called his name as he hit the last step, and after a resigned glance toward the parking lot, he came to her.

"Can I at least know why?" she asked, not wanting to beat around the bush. "I thought we had an amazing time."

The briefcase at his side twisted as he fidgeted — a very un-Drastos-like reaction. He slid his free hand into his pants pocket and stared at her with palpable frustration. She almost took a step back, unaccustomed to the non-congenial side of him.

"Whether the time was well-spent or not is of no importance. It is a matter of the future. We — you and I — cannot have one together. I take responsibility for leading you on, but there can be nothing between us," he said matter-of-factly.

It was an answer that sparked a million questions. "Why?"

His jaw tightened, and his shoulders lifted in an almost imperceptible shrug. "It's not something to discuss. It simply is, Ms. Harris." His voice lowered, and something akin to remorse entered his voice. "You can't know…"

"What? Like if you told me you'd have to kill me?" The ridiculous joke was out before she could think better of her tone.

Drastos tilted his head. "Yes."

She wanted to laugh, but one look at his face killed the urge. Everything about his demeanor chilled, and now he stared at her with ice in his eyes as if daring her to break the uncomfortable silence that had settled between them. Then he turned on his heel and walked away.

Chapter 2

Alyssa shivered as she stepped out of the tub into an impossibly cold bathroom. The small room should have been a fogged-up mess from her scalding-hot shower, but cool air drifted through the partially open door.

A door she had definitely closed before her shower.

Staring at the door, she wrapped a towel around her torso and pulled her shower cap off to free her curls. She lived alone, but anytime she used the room she still closed the door. Now she approached it silently and listened. Her pulse sped, jolted by the idea that somehow, she wasn't alone.

Closing her eyes, she flattened her body against the door and waited for any sound. Her apartment was absolutely silent.

She took a deep breath. Obviously, she hadn't pulled the door hard enough to latch. That had to be it. Now she was scaring herself over nothing. She opened the door wide and looked into her bedroom. It was empty—of course. No sign of anything out of place, although there was a mysterious chill in the air.

Air conditioner on the fritz? Had to be. She'd call her land-lord in the morning. Convinced her imagination was playing tricks, she dried off and slid into her satin robe for a lazy night of ice cream and binge-watching in bed. It still disappointed her that her great love affair with Drastos was over before it ever officially began. Drastos. His name still made her heart flutter. Damn him.

Was there a support group for women pining after unavailable, mysterious, foreign men? At least, she thought he was foreign, with a name like Drastos. Plus, after a few drinks, a strange accent would loosen from his tongue. She'd asked him about his unique name, accent, and where he was from, but he was impressively evasive. No matter. Curiosity be damned. She planned to purge him from her thoughts with endless rom-coms.

That plan died when she left her bedroom and found her living room window wide open. Night air blew through the screenless frame, causing her long gauzy curtains to dance like pale blue ghosts in the dark room. She took a quick step back and braced herself in the doorway, part of her trying to remember where she'd left her phone, part of her reasoning that she was on the fourth level of her apartment complex, which sat on a steep hill, no less. Intruders wouldn't—no, they couldn't—use the window.

She backed up and bumped into something solid. Her blood ran cold. With a shriek, she leapt to run away, but a hand closed around her wrist and yanked her back into the bedroom. She stumbled and landed on the floor. Wasting no time, she scuttled away from the tall figure and went for her nightstand. She was ninety percent certain her phone was on it, and if not, the massive metal flashlight in the top drawer could make an impressive weapon.

Before she could reach the nightstand, powerful hands lifted her from the carpet and flung her onto the bed. She bounced in the center of the mattress, a tangle of shaking limbs and long robe as she turned over to face her intruder. It wasn't human.

The sound of her distress echoed off the walls as she stared, horrified, at what her brain identified as a demon—and yet demons weren't real. She wanted to deny what she saw.

Slender horns coiled up and away from the demon's ridged brow line, which currently held an unreadable expression over glossy black eyes. His skin was a deep brick red that darkened to black at his temples, pointed ears, clawed fingers, and cloven feet. A black tail curled and swayed behind him, drawing her attention to it and the other hanging appendage in that general vicinity. He was naked, but she was too frightened to spend more than a split-second of her attention on it.

As far as she knew, there was only one reason for a naked demon to appear in a woman's room at night.

Words jammed in her throat, and only strangled sounds escaped her. She wanted to crab-walk backward on the bed, but her legs refused to cooperate. All she could do was sit and tremble and stare.

"I couldn't resist," the demon said, his voice startlingly familiar.

He approached the side of her bed and dragged one black claw along the comforter. Light from her bedside lamp caught a streak of silver hiding behind one of his horns; a glowing beacon against the rest of his sleek black hair.

It couldn't be.

"Here I am, and I can't take it back," the demon said in a thoughtful tone. "After two centuries of good behavior, I suppose I'm due an act of purely foolish, selfish indulgence."

Drastos?

Her fear still muted her and hot tears streamed down her cheeks as she stared at the demon. Her mind warred. If it was Drastos, should she be afraid? She wanted to believe he wouldn't hurt her. Yet he'd broken into her apartment. And he was naked.

Demons with good intentions would wear clothing, right?

You've officially lost it.

He snarled at the bright lamp as if just noticing it, then slammed the cheap thing to the ground in a crash of metal and glass. She flinched at the sound and violence, her mind reeling.

The demon bent forward and hooked his hands behind her knees to drag her toward him. As he drew her closer, she sucked in heavy breaths. She wanted desperately to believe she was imagining things, or that he was a man in a costume, but up close, she couldn't deny how real he was. Dark spots appeared along the edges of her vision as she gasped again and again. She was going to hyperventilate and pass out—maybe that would be for the best.

Leaning over her, the demon inhaled slowly and released a low growl. The darkness increased her fear, and she closed her eyes as her thoughts swarmed; a cacophony of potential last-ditch efforts. All of them required her to move, however, and she'd frozen stiff with terror.

He forced her chin up with his sharp fingertip, and she sensed his intent before his mouth landed on her. She resisted the kiss, her lips tight and unresponsive, but his hand circled her throat, the gentle pressure a threat she understood. She forced herself to relax and parted her lips in surrender.

Whatever she expected, this wasn't it. The demon's kiss was so strange and hungry that her fear dissolved into confusion. Curiosity guided her into motion, and her tongue slid over the sharp points of his teeth. However frightening the circumstance, the kiss itself was... magical. Familiar.

The voice. The silver streak of hair. Now, this kiss.

Her memory wouldn't fail her here—this kiss was comforting and passionate—the culmination of years of longing. The same kiss she'd had with Drastos the night of their date. But how?

His grip tightened around her throat, and he shoved her

back on the bed. Her eyes sprang open to meet the demon's black stare. His dark lips curled into a sneer.

"I can taste your indecision. Do you fight because I'm a monster? Or do you surrender like the sweet little slut your body wants to be?"

More out of reflex than any conscious decision, she pushed against his chest. He released her neck to catch her hands. With his fist around her wrists, he stretched her arms above her head and pinned her to the mattress. His free hand stroked her cheek. The dull tips of his black, clawed fingertips dragged across her skin, raising gooseflesh over her body as they skimmed down her collarbone to slip into the robe's front.

She licked her lips, wanting to speak, but unsure of what to say. If this demon was Drastos, he'd been keeping a secret identity for years—or as he'd just said, centuries. If she let on that she knew who he was, she wouldn't survive the night. He'd told her earlier. He told her he'd have to kill her.

Oh fuck.

It made sense. He couldn't know that she recognized him. Although…

"Wh-what are you going to do to me?" she asked. Her voice was so meek and shaky, she barely recognized it herself. Fear compounded as her eyes adjusted to the moonlight spilling through the glass balcony door.

His brow arched. "Why, I'm going to fuck you, of course." His fingers hooked the belt at her waist and tugged the knot. "Isn't that obvious?"

She swallowed, flinching as he pulled the end of the belt loose with a hard yank.

"And after? Will you—will you…" she trailed off, unable to continue. She didn't want to die tonight.

He flicked each side of the robe away from her body, exposing her completely. "After? Maybe there will be no after."

He nodded as if the plan pleased him. "Maybe I will keep you forever, my own little pet."

Would that be the end of the world? As opposed to dying, maybe not. Then again, what about her life? Her dreams? Her goals? Her fucking dissertation and all the time she'd already poured into it?

Death, or become a demon's sex pet.

This was never supposed to be a choice she had to make.

He caressed her breasts, sweeping his claws from one to the other in lazy, deliberate circles.

Squirming, she locked her knees together. If she could buy some time, then maybe… maybe… maybe what?

The demon leaned down and licked her jaw, the sensual action giving her a close-up view of the black horns that swept away from his face and another glimpse of the silver streak. This was Drastos. She no longer had a doubt.

How she felt about it was still a tumble of confusion and anxiety, but she clung to the tiny comfort. The demon you know, and all that.

"And I have no say in the matter?" she asked.

He chuckled, his lips touching her neck and bathing it in the heat of his breath. "Say all you want. Scream if you'd like. No one will hear you except me, and I happen to find your voice to be absolutely delicious."

His head lowered to capture a nipple with his lips. He sucked and nibbled, her pleasure undeniable as he teased the hardened bud with sharp teeth that were somehow careful. For all her fear in this moment, her attraction to Drastos overpowered it. Even in this demon form with dark red skin and claws, she wanted him. Perhaps she was even more aroused. Could fear heighten the pleasure? She didn't know what to expect; had no control, and that held its own enticement.

She writhed beneath him, and as he switched his attention

to her other breast, a moan escaped. Fuck. Her right nipple was always more sensitive than the left, nothing to be embarrassed of, and yet even with her life hanging in the balance, heat flooded her cheeks. As his tongue swirled and teased, her lower belly fluttered and she felt the hot rush of her arousal pooling, broadcasting exactly how he affected her.

Drastos bit down hard, infusing the pleasure with pain in a divine moment that made her gasp. The sound must have pleased him; he lifted his head to reveal a wicked smile. Gazing down her body, he cupped between her legs and sank one of his fingers into her wet folds.

Her body's response rippled upward, and her mouth shot open. Her nipples ached for more attention, and every part of her felt alive.

He groaned as he slid his finger in and out of her tight channel. "The things I want to do to you."

She whimpered, not at his words but at the way her hips wanted to buck against him. She wanted to ride him. He'd barely touched her, and already she was primed to go.

The bed creaked as he knelt beside her. He grabbed the discarded belt. After tying it around her wrists—an action she watched rather languidly—he looped it around a bedpost and wrapped the loose end around his hand. He jerked on the improvised lead. The satin belt was surprisingly strong and tugged her up the bed. She scooted back until he appeared satisfied with her position against the bedpost and a mound of pillows.

He joined her on the bed, crowding her on the full-size mattress. Her bed was far too small for demon intruders. His hand shook as if throwing dice, and dashed her thoughts away. He'd grabbed something. What from where? Perhaps from under the pillows, but Alyssa knew her bedroom, and she kept nothing there.

"What did you—Ah!"

41

Gaping down, she saw a small clamp on her left nipple. It hurt, and she thrashed and squeaked in protest while he looked on with clear, despicable delight. When he reached toward her again, she twisted away.

"No," she whined.

He didn't listen, and pinched a matching clamp to her very sensitive, already aching right nipple. The bright silver stood out against her brown skin, taunting her.

She howled at the sharp pain jolting through her body. She kicked and cursed, and it dawned on her that maybe she didn't want this—him—after all.

The mattress bounced as Drastos moved, but she couldn't open her eyes against the agony. He caught her kicking legs and opened them wide. He pressed her knees open against the mattress, and then he licked her wet slit with his hot, thick tongue.

Some of the pain subsided. Her breath caught in her throat as his powerful tongue wriggled against her opening. Oh, sweet kittens... His tongue was not human. It was wider, longer, and... oh. Forked.

He plunged his tongue inside and covered her mound with his hot mouth. His teeth scraped against her clit, making her buck, but he held her still while he tasted her.

Her eyes rolled back, and she exhaled in desperate moans. As she panted, her shaking breasts snapped her awareness back to the clamps that kept her hard and aching. The soreness became delicious when combined with the intense sensation of Drastos licking between her legs.

She was so close. He nipped at her folds, the brief grazing of his teeth tormenting her closer and closer to the edge.

"No," he hissed.

She opened her eyes and strained to look down. He shook his head and sat up, abandoning her at the precipice of bliss.

"Not yet."

"What? Why?" she demanded.

He dug his claws into her thigh, enough to make her wince. "You exist for my pleasure, not the other way around."

She bit her lip to stifle her bubbling argument.

Rising from the bed, he looked her over. For a split second, as he shifted, his erection loomed at the edge of her vision.

It made sense for a seven-foot demon to have a proportional dick. However, the shadowy blur seemed far larger than warranted.

His hand churned a slow circle in the air, and from the shadows, he retrieved something. He brought it into a sliver of moonlight. At first glance, it looked to be a weapon. A curved sword.

Darkness bled through the edges of her vision.

Chapter 3

Drastos tapped Alyssa's cheek. "Scared?"

Her vision focused. Moonlight wrapped around the edges of the object he held, and he turned it slowly in the light to show her.

Not a weapon. A... well, she wasn't entirely sure. It had a handle like a sword, but the part that would be a blade appeared to be more like—her eyes widened—a dildo?

"What is that?" she shrieked.

"I came prepared."

"But—"

"It's a courtesy," he said in a warning tone. "Your body wasn't made to accommodate me, pet. Though it would all feel the same to me, I thought you might not want me to rip you apart during our fun."

"W-with that you—"

He chuckled softly. "It's an usveis." The sound rolled from his tongue, sounding infinitely more poetic than the object appeared. "It's a training wand, of sorts."

"Training?"

"Sometimes humans are kept. Whether for pleasure, enter-

45

tainment, or breeding, an usveis is the best way to acclimate a human to the variety of demon genitalia." His brows lowered, and he stared at the wand in his grip. "This will prepare your sweet cunt for me."

A chill ran through her, and she stared at the usveis. It was hard to see any details in the dark, as the wand was equally dark. She could make out the frightening length and girth thicker than both her wrists together, and that it wasn't smooth at all, but covered in ridges and bumps that she'd never have imagined on a male appendage. And he implied he was larger? That this was just to make her ready? Her eyes strayed down, but his back was to the window, hiding the front of his body in shadows.

He yanked her legs to him so one hung over the side of the bed, then pressed the wand to her entrance.

Grabbing her face, he forced her to look at him as he teased the head of the unexpectedly warm usveis up and down her slit, coating it with her arousal. Her brows furrowed as its tip slid inside, her teeth gritted in uncertainty and anticipation. Drastos grinned at her reaction.

"It's difficult, this restraint," he whispered, "when every instinct of mine is to bury myself into you, regardless of your pain or anger. You're the only woman to see my gentle side."

Her mouth opened to remark on his "gentleness" but as if to prove her point, he pushed the wand deeper, giving her a feel of the first hard ridge at the top of the shaft. She released a soft sound. The sensation wasn't terrible, but unexpected.

She stared into his dark gaze and imagined a human Drastos looking back at her. She loved his mahogany eyes and thick, ever-serious brows. While at work, he always had a look of severe concentration. Over the years, she'd prided herself on breaking him down and making him smile and laugh.

The shaft slipped out before plunging farther in, another ridge notching against the top of her opening and reminding her of how long it had been since she'd been with a man. She was wet and aroused, but still too tight.

He pulled the wand back and pushed it in with more force. Her body opened to it, and this time the ridges were a textured glide that felt divine. Her lips parted, and she moaned softly.

Pleasure and the full sensation of the usveis sinking deeper and deeper worked her into a heady trance. Drastos worked the usveis slow and then fast and then slow again, his expression tight as he kept his eyes on her face the entire time. The pressure of the girthy wand against her walls wasn't unpleasant, and even the keen stretch became bliss as her body adjusted. The usveis worked like magic.

"Now we begin," he said.

She blinked at him. Begin? Her body was taking the full length of the wand, and it felt like a perfect fit. Unless he meant to begin with the actual sex? She couldn't ask, as her climax loomed just out of reach, and she grasped desperately for it.

The usveis undulated within her, and she froze.

"What's happening?" she squeaked.

He thrust the wand deeper inside, burying it until the round handle pressed against her opening. The usveis pulsated and trembled against her walls. The sensation transformed; starting pleasant, becoming strange and mildly uncomfortable, then reaching the brink of pain.

"No-no-no," she moaned. "No more!"

Her arms shook, and she yanked at the satin tethering her against her bedpost. She groaned and squirmed, which only made it worse. Her stomach cramped, and she kicked in panic, nearly causing herself to slide from the bed.

Drastos pressed the hilt of the usveis upward, and it molded against the top of her mound like warm wax. He kissed her, and though she was trembling with fear and pain, the taste of him still dazed her. The kiss regulated her breathing, and she tried to calm her limbs, which still wanted to thrash and seek a means of escape.

He spoke against her lips, "This is for your own good. Let it happen. Allow the pain to become pleasure."

The doubt must have been clear on her face, because he cupped her chin and kissed her again, his tongue gently sweeping against hers. Between her legs, the hilt of the usveis tingled against her clit. Drastos groaned and twisted the handle, causing the shaft to cease its wild movements and slow into a firm undulation that was easier to bear. Her body still cramped, but as his reassurance sank in, a wave of relief swept over her.

Gradually, the pressure against her inner walls lost its harsh edge and became not only bearable but gratifying.

"Oh my… f-fuck," she cried out as she convulsed around the squirming wand.

Spasms struck her inner walls, tugging loose her ability to think straight. Pleasure unlike anything she'd known churned through her, and she begged through lips dry from panting.

"Please, please, yes…"

"Not yet."

Chapter 4

She grunted in frustration. He was controlling her climax. She didn't know or care how, but she knew it was his doing that kept her wound tight and unable to find release.

The hilt of the usveis loosened from her body, no longer molded to fit perfectly against her mound. Drastos eased the wand out slowly, moving in the tiniest, most tormenting increments as her walls clutched to hold it in. Alyssa could make out a teasing expression on his faintly moonlit face, as if he felt exactly how her body reacted.

The tip of the wand left her, immediately flooding her with an empty ache. Drastos gestured, and the usveis disappeared. If she weren't on the edge of madness from craving her orgasm, she may have questioned him.

Her chest rose and fell with her heavy breathing. He swept a heated touch up her thigh and let out a primal rumble.

A sense of urgency hung in the air, a buzzing awareness that prickled at her skin; yet somehow, time had slowed, prolonging the moment as he moved closer. Between the passing seconds, she pictured how the next part of the night would go. She was ready for him physically, but his earlier threat still lingered in the back of her mind. He hadn't promised she'd be safe.

He loomed over her, his form encased in shadow. "Don't do that."

"Do what?"

"I can taste your fear. One moment, you were deliciously eager." As he spoke, he moved between her legs. "You shouldn't fear this, not now."

He was ready to plunge into her even though she reeked of fear, and she wanted to stall. She could ask him what he planned to do with her at the end of the night and perhaps get a more straightforward answer than, "maybe you'll be my pet."

He was a demon. He was exactly what nightmares were made of—or maybe he was supposed to be. Her perception of him was biased between the pleasure he'd given her and her belief that he was—somewhere deep down, beneath his fire and brimstone exterior—still the guy she'd had gushy romantic daydreams about for the past few years.

"Why do you care now?" she asked, the words rushing from her. "Earlier you said I could scream all I wanted. Why does my fear matter now?"

He growled, and she sensed frustration in him she couldn't comprehend. She had her own tangled emotions to deal with, and she couldn't begin to imagine his.

The broad head of his cock pushed into her silencing her wandering mind and questions. He wasn't open to discussion after all.

She hissed as he entered her, his hard flesh rubbing her tender walls and blending pain with pleasure. She struggled against her bindings. Her body yearned to move and adjust to more easily take him, but her arms were bound fast to the bedpost.

He slid a hand behind her and pulled her to the edge of the

bed. He worked his length in and out of her wet heat in slow, torturous strokes. She wanted him. She wanted more. And if it hurt, she wanted it harder.

Rather than fight her strange thoughts, she closed her eyes and lifted her hips farther, leveraging her weight by digging one heel into the bed.

"Yes," he moaned. "Let me in. More."

The bed creaked, and the mattress shifted with his forceful thrusts. He snarled in frustration, and in the next moment, she found herself lifted from the bed. The belt around her wrists fell loose for a second as he readjusted and with a yank, he tightened it once more, securing her arms higher above her. She wrapped her legs around his waist, and he held her weight with one spread hand beneath her.

Gravity took hold, and she sank fully onto his cock. She cried out at the shocking sensation of him filling her and bottoming out. Leave it to a demon to make cervix slamming a turn-on.

He thrust in and out of her, finding a steady rhythm as she bounced against him and enjoyed the ride. It was the most vigorous, satisfying sex she'd ever had while doing nothing. She was being used, but it was damned enjoyable. From a dark corner of her mind came the thought that maybe, just maybe, being his sex toy forever wouldn't be the worst fate.

The feel of him changed from one moment to the next, his shaft smooth one pulse and rough the next. It wasn't the right time to ask, and she was certain she couldn't form words. Her brain was absolute jelly, and all she wanted was to chase down the pleasure of his body ramming into hers.

He must have needed this. Though she couldn't know his motivation, she understood this maddening desire to let lust rein and give in to their carnal needs. Regardless of what this meant to him, for her, it was the culmination of dirty thoughts, teasing dreams, and a never-ending fantasy of taking Drastos to her bed. She'd earned every moment of this fantasy and its included pleasure.

Her climax loomed with a tension stronger than ever before. Drastos was close too, judging by his grunts and the increasingly aggressive way he squeezed her bottom and yanked her to him with each thrust. The outward drag of his cock from her body became tighter. Rougher. As if it didn't want to leave her. Prominent ridges swelled along his shaft and pressed against her walls, filling her with concern and overwhelming exhilaration.

"Please," she whispered. "Let me…"

"Yes," he snarled. "Come for me. I want to feel your cunt squeezing me as I pump you full of my seed."

At his words, a shudder tore through her. In her wildest dreams, she couldn't imagine proper, suited Drastos saying such things to her, and yet they were perfect in this moment, propelling her into the spiraling chaos of orgasm.

He plunged harder, and deeper, and she shattered into a million pieces of herself. Denied climax so many times, the built-up pleasure exploded again and again until she was dizzy and screaming with rapture.

Through her euphoria, she felt his cock throb deep within her. It seemed to expand until it filled her completely, then rumbling groans shook through his chest and vibrated against her, heralding his release. Heat flooded her, and he cradled her through it all, through every tremble of his body in hers.

Before the waves of pleasure died down, he released her from the bedpost, untied her arms, and threw her on the bed again. Now that she had the freedom, she reveled in the feel of his hot skin beneath her palms. She stroked his chest and arms, then dragged her nails down his back as he pistoned into her with wild abandon. Demons weren't hindered by release, she noted. Would this go all night?

The bed groaned in protest beneath them, and she grinned, considering how much a demon must weigh. She kicked at the blankets, trying to find purchase to lift her hips to him again, by now knowing exactly what she needed. When his thrusts hit too deep, she squirmed instinctively away, and he held her down, pinning her against the mattress.

She couldn't budge him and was effectively trapped, yet she felt safe. His muscles bunched beneath her hands, his effort shaking them both. He was in a frenzy, and she held on for the ride. He pumped into her again and again, and once more she felt him pulsate and release within her.

Chapter 5

Alyssa's breathing gradually evened, but she clung to the lingering sensations swirling through her body. Never could she have imagined a passion that would test and challenge her like this. Fear and pain, hope and ecstasy had blended in strange juxtaposition.

He withdrew from her slowly and bent to trail kisses from her neck downward. He stopped at her breasts and licked her sore nipple. She'd forgotten the small clamps he'd placed there, the sensation lost in the sea of blissful ecstasy he'd given her throughout the night. He freed her nipples now; removed the clamp and drew the aching bud into his mouth. His tongue swirled and teased, igniting her blood. He bit down, and she whimpered at the pain, but it didn't deter him. She bled beneath his sharp teeth; small pricks of white-hot pain chased by the sweet relief of pleasure.

He repeated the action on her left breast, then moved up. Hovering over her on strong arms, he gazed down at her, his expression unreadable, yet comforting.

Unbidden, the memory of her first meeting with Drastos unfolded in her mind. She'd been flustered and overwhelmed, and the librarian at the checkout station had pointed her to Drastos' desk at the center of the East wing in the vast university library. She'd begun rambling to him immediately about her research, ideas, and what she needed help with, and he'd made short, scratchy notes on a pad while he listened patiently.

When she ran out of breath, he offered suggestions. That was the moment she opened her eyes and truly saw him. Freed from the madness of her upcoming paper—due three months from then, but she was easily stressed—she blinked and absorbed the handsome face staring at her. His soothing, strangely accented voice drifted across her ears like a refreshing mist.

She'd made it through all of her school years without developing a serious crush on anyone, but Drastos hit her like an arrow straight to the chest. He took up residence in her heart, and from that day forward, she'd become ever more enamored. After a while, it seemed mutual.

And he'd come to her tonight. It had to mean something. Even if that something was no more than a night of meaningless, mind-blowing fucking, she'd take it.

"Drastos," she said with a heavy, languid sigh.

The demon, who remained hovering over her in the after-glow, went still. She flinched, realizing her mistake.

"What?" he asked.

She shook her head.

He gripped her chin and forced her to look straight at him. "You knew."

Dim moonlight slid along one side of his face, scarcely illuminating his dark skin. She couldn't read his expression, hidden as he was, and no amount of staring solved that.

"I won't tell anyone. I won't say anything."

His grip on her face tightened briefly but soon released. His clawed thumb stroked her cheek. "Did you know the entire time?"

"Yes," she admitted. "Or, I just guessed. I…"

"How?"

She imagined where the telltale patch of silver hair hid and reached up to touch it. Her fingers brushed the ridged horn curling up from his left temple. She traced past it and twirled the hidden hair forward.

He let out a low rumble. Though she sensed it wasn't in anger, she flinched.

"Just that?" he asked. "A lock of hair?"

She almost nodded, but that wasn't the truth. The truth was embarrassing, but his secret was out in the open. Keeping her own felt petty. "And the kiss. I remember the way you kiss."

"You recall that?"

"Of course. That kiss was amazing," she said somewhat defensively. "When you've been waiting forever for something, you savor it. Cherish it. I don't think I could ever forget that kiss."

"It meant that much?"

She hesitated, and then her voice came out shaky and small. "It did. So much."

The room gradually brightened. Turning her head, she found the source was the remaining lamp on her other nightstand humming to life, twin to the one he'd smashed earlier. The warm glow flickered and grew, casting enough light to reveal to the top of his body, down to where her legs wrapped around his waist. She looked into his eyes and wanted to ask how he turned on the light without his hands, but then again, he was a demon. A demon who had slipped into a fourth-level apartment through the window. A demon who could summon a sex toy from thin air and make it vanish just as easily.

"I can keep a secret," she said, breaking the silence.

"This doesn't bother you?" he arched a brow and gestured to his face.

Her initial fear had long since faded. Red or not, demon or not, he was still attractive, however different.

"Would it be going out on a limb to assume that to other demons, you're considered hot?" she asked.

He shrugged. "To other Maelificars, yes. I've turned a few succubi's heads as well. Incubi, too."

She let that slide, not wanting to get distracted. She considered him; her gaze drifting down his muscular torso. "You're handsome in this form. As handsome as when you appear human."

"Truly?" he asked, amused.

Biting her lip, she gave a quick nod. "The horns. The mystery. The danger. But then again, you're looking at a girl who always had a soft spot for the bad guy in scary movies. Watching Labyrinth always made me feel funny."

Drastos chuckled and shifted beside her. He stared at her for a moment, then fell onto his back. The bed shook under his large body as he settled onto a pillow and looked up to the ceiling. It was strange to see him this way, laying in her bed and taking up most of it. The sight of the intimidating demon laying against her lavender sheets was almost comical.

"Humans are fascinating," he mused.

"We are," she agreed. She pulled the rumpled blanket from the foot of the bed and brought it over her body. The apartment had a chill. "What now?"

He didn't respond, and continued to look up.

She tried to be patient, reasoning he was just as unprepared for this outcome as she was.

"We aren't meant to form attachments to humans," he said finally. "For a multitude of reasons."

"Why did you ever agree to a date, then?" she asked.

"I thought it would go poorly. I thought that the reality would pale compared to the imagined 'what if' world we'd created around ourselves. Years of flirting. Of getting to know each other. It meant nothing because we'd never dug deeper."

"Is that the truth, then? Did it go poorly?" She braced for his answer.

He exhaled audibly. "It was a disaster. Everything that drew me to you in the first place compounded. I realized I'd miscalculated before we'd even made it to the restaurant. The connection between us was genuine, and by the time we had that kiss—the one you feel so strongly about—I knew I had to have you."

Her heart raced. The emotions she tried to stifle returned tenfold. She could make sense of things now. He had to reject her, or thought he had to.

"I thought if I came tonight and had you, that would be enough."

"And now?"

"We walk among humans daily. Have done so for years. You aren't the first to discover the truth."

"And I assume that usually means... silencing them."

He gave her a look that confirmed her guess. "Or they were brought into servitude in our home realm, in one fashion or another. Human servants in Pandəmonium aren't uncommon." He growled and left the bed. "But that won't be your fate."

She sat up, holding the blanket against her chest for comfort more than modesty. "Earlier you said—"

"I recall. I meant to scare you, for my sake. You were supposed to be afraid of me. Hate me. Make it easier for this to happen once and be no more than a nightmare that would fade in your memory." He paced back and forth, his tail flicking with annoyance.

"I guess there's no demonic memory wiping ability?" she asked. Not that she wanted her memory erased.

He shook his head. "Madness. We can inflict madness and then your memories would be a muddle. That's as close as it gets. Plucking out individual moments is an impossible task for Maelificars such as myself."

Maelificars? Her face scrunched, but he continued past her confusion, "Other demons can do it, but it isn't the sort of favor one asks for."

"Then…" She couldn't imagine what that left.

"There are rules. Pandamonium is chaos incarnate, but all demons bend to order in some fashion. An unclaimed human with knowledge of the truth can't simply run free. I must claim responsibility for my actions. For you, there is only one fate."

The solemn finality of his words swept over her. So far, the presented options were death, madness, or servitude. He wouldn't kill her. She was certain of that. It didn't seem he wanted to drive her mad, and he'd implied he wouldn't bring her to Pandamonium.

Approaching the bed, he held out his hand. She took it without hesitation, and when he gently tugged, she stood before him, allowing the blanket to fall away. His pitch-black eyes roamed her naked body a moment before meeting hers.

"Join me in eternity?" he asked.

"Wha—what?"

His hand squeezed hers, and he pulled her toward him until her sore breasts collided against his muscled stomach.

He loomed over her, reminding her exactly how large and intimidating he could be.

He wound a lock of her hair around his dark claws. "Marry me."

Epilogue

Alyssa wrinkled her brow and pondered the glowing numbers on her microwave. It was three-seventeen in the morning, but she was craving hot cocoa. The microwave would make considerably less noise than a whistling kettle. Or maybe if she babysat the kettle, she could catch it right before it whistled —

"You should be in bed," a deep voice growled behind her.

She jolted back, landing against a hard, familiar chest. She looked up to Drastos' human face — a face she couldn't see because she was lurking around the kitchen in the dark — but a face she knew had a sour, disapproving expression.

"I'm still working."

"No," he disagreed. "I know you. When you're up this late 'working,' it means you're staring at the same information and rewording it again and again until you're exhausted and feeling 'snacky', as you call it."

She rolled her eyes and pushed away from him to flick on the light, since they were both up anyhow. "I do some of my best work at night."

"You believe that, but trust me, it isn't true. You're just

61

confused because the work that keeps you awake would put everyone else to sleep," he grumbled. "Data organization optimization."

Shaking her head, she leaned against the doorjamb. "But I'm awake. I may as well attempt to be productive." She arched a brow at him. "You should find my work interesting. It's directly related to how easily you do your work. The university library's search engine is atrocious."

"I have advantages that nullify the barriers of an average human researcher," he countered.

She grabbed the kettle, her desire for a hot drink rekindled. His hand gripped her wrist and tugged, making her release the kettle.

"You and your night cravings," he chided.

"Don't say it that way. They aren't that sort of cravings."

He smirked, and his eyes flickered to her stomach. She wasn't expecting, but it was always on their minds, as it wasn't for lack of enthusiastic trying.

"If they were 'that sort,' they wouldn't be as mundane as your usual nighttime foraging."

"In any case—" She freed her hand from his and gestured to the stove. "I was just going to boil some water for cocoa."

"I suppose that's better than the time I found you frying bacon at two in the morning and eating it right out of the pan."

She bit her lip, fighting the blush that accompanied her embarrassment at being caught. Most people grabbed a handful of chips or microwaved pizza rolls when they got the munchies at night. She'd once cooked a New York strip and called it a snack. In her defense, she was usually so busy during the day that she skipped lunch and rushed through dinner. Her mundane was another's unthinkable, and yet she guessed that demon baby cravings would be on an entirely different level.

"If you can't sleep, I can remedy that," he said. His eyes met hers, and as she watched, his mahogany irises darkened into the pitch-black that signaled his demon form coming forth.

She was over his shoulder within a blink, and back in their bedroom the next. Since their whirlwind marriage last year, they'd moved into his home—a luxurious, multilevel brownstone that put her tiny apartment to shame.

With the new home came front row seats to the double life Drastos lived. His friends were mostly Maelificars, but she'd also met a pair of incubi and a few vampyrs. He enjoyed hosting them, turning from mild-mannered research librarian by day, to debauched demon millionaire by night. Or as she liked to put it, librarian in the stacks, demon in the sack. She loved both sides endlessly.

He tossed her onto the bed and flexed, shredding his onyx silk pajamas in a violent transformation to his demon form, sans the wings she'd discovered after their first night together.

The wings were a surprise he'd shown her later, and were functional, giving him the ability to teleport short distances in the human world, and between this realm and his home—Pandæmonium, the demon realm. They were cumbersome, and he often left them off when he transformed, just as he nixed the tail if he pulled his demon form out and wanted to don demon-appropriate attire. The latter had occurred a few times thanks to some very interesting dinner parties at their home.

It turned out that demons were fine with human companions as long as there was true commitment. Marriage made her acceptable, because demons could not break contracts, and there was no divorce for the supernatural. Actually, she had a suspicion that not even death would do them part, but she had yet to find the right moment to delve into what would likely be a deep and dark philosophical discussion.

He joined her on the bed, which didn't creak like her old one. His was a monstrously large and sturdy bed with a black-lacquered frame she suspected was made from center cuts of a tree. She'd seen no bed as massive, but it was necessary to accommodate his demon form. However expensive, it was a practical choice. The night before their wedding he'd visited her apartment for nostalgia's sake and her frame had splintered and cracked beneath his vigorous movements. It wasn't a moment she wanted to repeat.

From beneath the cage of his body, she eased out of her robe and tossed it aside, relishing the way his gaze wandered over her nude body. She slept naked these days, a demand of his that she had grown comfortable with.

He lowered himself until his chest pressed against hers, the warmth of his body quickly seeping into her. Their lips met, followed by the heady rush that always accompanied his kisses —she hoped it never faded. The taste of his lips and tongue imparted giddy magic on her. She moaned into him, and he swallowed the sound and followed it with a possessive growl that rumbled through them both.

Pulling back, he sucked her lower lip between his teeth and gently bit down until she squeaked from the tiny, sharp pain.

"I love that sound. I could devour you."

His words vibrated along her skin, filling her with anticipation. His arms straightened, lifting his heavy body from hers. She resisted the temptation to lie back and welcome his wicked, talented tongue. Instead, she licked her lips and gazed meaningfully down his body. "I want to do the devouring."

He grinned. "Are you certain?"

"I'm feeling snacky," she teased, and pushed against his chest.

He rolled over rather dramatically and fell to his back as if she had overpowered him. He was no longer semi-aroused but full-blown erect. She crawled to his side and wrapped her hand around the impressive length, eager to try her hand at pleasing him this way.

Frequent, vigorous sex and some sort of subtle demon mysticism helped her lower body accommodate him, but throats didn't work the same way.

As her doctorate proved, Alyssa was not a quitter.

Determination filled her in tandem with the surge of lust that hummed through her from the sight of Drastos, naked and waiting for her mouth.

She pressed a kiss to the broad head of his eager, twitching cock. Drastos tapped the leg closest to him, signaling her to change places. His preferred position involved placing herself in what she'd previously seen as an undignified position. Marriage to a demon had cured her of most of her inhibitions, however, so she straddled his muscular chest and settled over him.

He was roughly two feet taller than her, making mutual oral impossible, but he liked to see and play with her when she went down on him. True to habit, he gently sunk a clawed fingertip into her before she'd reclaimed her hold. She closed her eyes and enjoyed his teasing. His claws weren't razor sharp but dulled. Still, they could rip and tear. It was like being fucked with a weapon. She'd embraced the madness of her choice in wedding a demon, though, and didn't fear his touch. He'd never hurt her without bringing pleasure in excess.

Opening her eyes, she wrapped both hands around him and felt the texture of his shaft change. In the early stages of arousal, it was smooth, but he was already past that, anxious as he was for her mouth.

She licked the mushroomed crown and trailed her tongue up and down his length, feeling the ridges hidden beneath his dark skin become prominent. She squeezed her hand around his base and pumped up, causing the ridges to retreat. Once he neared climax, they'd remain raised and hard, making withdrawal rough. Drastos had explained that demon mating was feistier than humans', and their anatomy reflected that. On the same vein, male demons enjoyed oral sex so much that their cocks didn't engorge to full size if stimulated by a mouth. Drastos was still huge, but by comparison he was currently, theoretically, manageable.

Spit trickled from her tongue as she laved him, coating him to ease her efforts. Once satisfied, she wrapped her lips around his crown and sucked gently. A guttural groan rumbled behind her, filling her with bubbly delight. She sank further down, taking him inch by thick inch.

She'd never managed to deepthroat him before, but felt lucky tonight. Bobbing slowly up and down, her hands mimicking her motion lower down his shaft, she enjoyed the feel of him and his salty pre-spend. He worked two fingers into her, and the distraction helped her sink into the hypnotic headspace she needed.

His cock flexed at the back of her throat. She didn't gag, but the sensation was uncomfortable. Of all the lessons she'd learned in her sexual adventures with Drastos, the key was that rough, passionate sex rarely looked pretty. She had to accept the tears and sweat—and in this case, the tears and drooling and choking—to reach nirvana. She half-whimpered as she sank down on him. Each determined bob sent him deeper than he'd ever been before, and closer to her dark fantasy.

Before her lips met her hands, she pulled back with a gasp. Lips parted, she breathed heavily against him, catching her breath. Her head spun and her ears rang.

"Fuck," Drastos groaned.

His voice was muffled as if he spoke through water. She was in her own world. Her skin tingled, charged with chaotic, lust-driven energy. She took him into her mouth again, deeper. His length slid against the walls of her throat and sent a ripple of awareness through her. Going down on him wasn't his pleasure alone. She was dripping wet for him.

She moaned, and the vibration made his cock jerk. Drastos shook beneath her.

"Mine," he snarled.

Drastos

THERE WAS NOTHING QUITE LIKE A SULTRY WOMAN'S THROAT clamping and moaning around one's cock to snap the tether of self-control.

Drastos' neck arched back as a shudder ran through him. Alyssa wanted this. She wanted to suck him dry. It was her fantasy, her terms. However, he was a demon. He would take control. It was inevitable.

She'd pushed him over the edge, and he was no longer satisfied to lie back and toy with her sweet cunt while she worked her magic and worshipped his cock. He wanted to fuck her pretty mouth and force her to swallow every drop of his seed —take what he wanted.

Reaching down, he buried his hand in her thick black curls. Mesmerized by the sight of her glistening wet cunt, he guided her head up and down in the perfect rhythm, feeding his desire for control. Her throat was a vise, and he gritted his teeth at the tight sensation on the sensitive ridges along his length. She was too perfect. He didn't deserve this, and yet he'd make the most of it because he was a greedy demon.

Her hand pressed into his thigh, and she rose slightly. The movement distracted him, and he gripped her arm to hold her where he wanted. He pushed her head back down through the resistance. Deeper, faster. His eyes clenched shut, and he focused only on the feel of gliding in and out of her throat. Spit trickled down his sac. She was nearing her limit. So was he.

He held her hair and pushed her all the way down. His hips flexed and arched up—he couldn't help it. He held her shaking body as he used her mouth, fucking her throat in rough desperation.

Their marital union formed a mental bond between them, and though he rarely pried into her thoughts or emotions, she was mentally screaming at the moment. She would black out, and her body was panicking, but she didn't want him to stop. He would, however, hurry.

With a last shove, her soft lips hit the base of his shaft, and he threw his head back and roared. A wildfire of pleasure tunneled through his spine and exploded, sending hot jets of his seed down her welcoming throat. With the ecstasy came over-whelming dizziness, and though his cock still twitched and spilled, he yanked Alyssa free.

She gasped for breath, but the magnitude of his climax— she could rival a succubus for the way she drained and satisfied him—left him slow to recover.

At least, his brain was slow—his cock, not so much.

Gazing at his limp little wife sent another wave of urgent desire through him, and soon he was cradling her to him and easing himself into her wet and ready cunt. Her walls fluttered against him, and she gave a feeble protest that melted into sultry moans when he cupped between her legs and teased her swollen clit. He would make her come, feel her convulse on his shaft again and again… then tuck her into bed and hold her through the night. In the morning, he'd make her tea for her sore throat. Once she'd recovered, he'd be her soundboard as she talked through the plans and complications of her database project. He'd take her again the next night, of course. His need for her was insatiable, and he was only ever able to withdraw from her because he knew she wasn't going anywhere. He'd have her every day and night forever, never tiring.

They had rushed into marriage. No talk of feelings or weight on the decision made to keep her safe, in case their unsanctioned relationship was discovered. Day by day, it became clear that there was more between them than sex and practicality. Their relationship wasn't one of convenience or compromise, but of love.

Love.

Like most demons, Drastos was skeptical of it at first. Yet it turned out to be the ultimate aphrodisiac.

Trained By Incubus

Chapter 1

Vinos

Humans milled along the path in search of entertainment, and I followed, appraising them for the pleasures they offered. Corsets lifted breasts into bountiful platters and tight leggings showcased perfectly round bottoms made for spanking. As far as possibilities, I was drowning in them. Any of the beautiful women could make for a delightful toy, but I hadn't been able to decide.

"What in chaos are you doing?" a sharp tone berated me, and I groaned, recognizing the source.

I glanced to my right, where a curvy redhead with furious blue eyes and deceptively angelic freckles stood. Dressed head-to-toe in skin-tight leather, Naeve was—to my guess—dressed as a sexy assassin. Not the usual costume found at a Renaissance festival, but it still managed to work. Largely because her body was made for display.

"If it isn't my favorite succubus," I drawled, walking to meet her.

She snarled, and for a moment her sharp fangs showed before morphing back to pearly-white human teeth. She grabbed my arm and pulled me away from the path and around the side of a building selling swords and other medieval-inspired weaponry. "Vinos. Have you lost your damned mind?"

Before I replied, Therris, my partner-in-crime for the evening, appeared behind Naeve and wrapped his arms around her waist possessively. The fresh spark of red anger in her eyes suggested that Therris was pressing his erection against her ass. She spun and gripped the lapels of the black vest he wore over his bare chest.

"I'll rip it off," she said with a menacing snarl. She glanced between the two of us. "Explain yourselves."

I shrugged and reached up to pat the small horns that protruded from my forehead. "Easier than buying a costume."

"Relax," Therris said. He slid away from Naeve and adjusted himself subtly in the thin, baggy pants he wore. "It's not like we've never done this before."

"If you can't tell the difference between Halloween night and the middle of the fucking day in summer, you need a new brain." She gestured toward us. "You can't wear your demon skin and mingle this closely with humans in broad daylight."

I disagreed, but it was pointless to argue. By our nature, incubi and succubi were incompatible, and this meant most of our interactions involved annoying each other. It was an inherent imperative, a decision made by the higher powers so that the two races wouldn't fuck non-stop every time they crossed paths. The decision had been swiftly made after setting loose the first succubi and incubi into the world; instead of seducing humans, the demons had embarked on a months-long orgy.

Naeve's appearance turned me on, but I'd get a killer migraine and vomit if I tried to bang her. Therefore, her presence was a waste of time.

"Are you even listening?" she asked.

"No," I admitted. "We're here to find a toy. I assume you are as well. Why don't you go do that and leave us alone?"

"If a Maelificar sees you—"

"You think any royalty—masquerading as human or not— would set foot here? They would get mud on their designer shoes," Therris interjected. "We aren't insipid. Just horny."

She shook her head. "Fine. It's your hides if you end up in the hole."

She shot each of us one last look of disgust before swaggering off. I watched her round bottom sway back and forth, mildly impressed that she walked with such confidence in sky-high stilettos without breaking an ankle on the uneven dirt and rock path.

"Do we want something like that?" Therris asked, his pitch-black eyes following the succubus as she disappeared into a tavern.

"No." I skimmed the crowd, ignoring the women who tried to meet my eyes and smile. The insatiable hunger for sex had risen in the presence of the succubus and gave me a better idea. "I want the opposite."

"Slim, then." Therris gave a nod.

We returned to the path which herded the humans like cattle from storefront to storefront, attraction to attraction, assessing their potential prey. The humans were like pretty flowers stamped across the scenery, none standing out.

Therris stopped and tapped my arm. Lifting his chin, he indicated a young woman perusing a booth that sold handmade jewelry. While most of the humans moved in groups, she was alone. That would make it easier if we chose her.

Long chestnut hair cascaded down her back, and I smiled, imagining the silky strands wrapped around my fist. She studied a necklace, and when she held it up in examination, I noticed her lithe figure. Small breasts. Small waist and hips. Tall with long legs. She had an athletic look, even though she wore a bright blue medieval dress with long bell sleeves.

We moved to the booth, and as we approached, she noticed us with wide golden-brown eyes. She wore no makeup, and her facial features were strong, not soft.

It wasn't only her appearance that called to me, however. An incubus had visited her in the past, though the mark was faint. A year, perhaps more, had passed to allow the bond to fade to its current level.

"One of yours?" I asked Therris.

Therris shook his head.

"Perfect," I whispered.

Chapter 2

Emma

"Perfect."

"It's always the unassuming ones that have the most wicked desires."

They spoke over me, whoever they were. I didn't recognize them.

I was coming out of sleep the way a lucky mammoth would pull out of tar, and as I struggled to open my damn eyes, each spoken consonant thumped inside my head, an ache reminiscent of the pain I'd gotten from listening to business calls while hungover. But this wasn't the case. No way the tiny cups of overpriced festival mead had knocked me out.

A tremor of fear pierced my consciousness. Had I been drugged?

I had been looking at necklaces and then... and then what?

Something touched my shoulder and my entire body jolted in surprise. Then finally—finally—my eyes opened.

I regretted opening them. Each blink shed awareness on a new facet of the hell I'd woken in. I shivered against a cold floor of black tiles. The cold made me look down. I was naked.

My muscles were sluggish, hindering my attempt to stand, and when I managed to get my feet beneath me, the restraints I hadn't noticed around my wrists violently hindered my upward momentum. Shoulders aching, I crouched and examined the cuffs for a latch, but they were wide leather with no visible way of opening them. The wrist cuffs were tethered to each other about six inches apart, and together they attached to a long, leather lead that was secured to the floor near me.

The length was enough for me to kneel over the eyelet bolt and lift my arms to my face. I yanked at it with every ounce of strength I had. Once. Twice. Again and again while cursing and hoping, not expecting it to break but still overcome by frustration when it didn't. My arms shook, the muscles numbing from the strain.

"Don't hurt yourself."

The words froze me completely, stilling my actions as well as turning my blood into icy slush. My stomach turned, and it occurred to me that before I'd woken, I'd heard voices. Two of them. My head was a foggy mess, but I assumed this voice was one of the same as from before. One of my captors, then.

I looked around me. I hadn't given my surroundings much attention. Waking naked and tethered, possibly recovering from being roofied, those things took priority. I took the room in now as I searched for the source of the voice. The black floor tiles met with matching paneling, and ornate crystal chandeliers hung above. They cast too much light, drawing my eyes to the furniture scattered throughout the expansive room.

My breath caught as I noticed the straps or cuffs that seemed to adorn every strange article. The room was a dungeon, but instead of being dark and seedy, it was brightly lit and spacious, like a ballroom.

Beneath my fear ran a torrent of something else—something I wanted to stuff down and forget about but couldn't. Heat swept through me and I shook my head, trying to remind myself that I was in danger. But curiosity won. My imagination reached out to my surroundings, painting a depraved fantasy that didn't care that I'd been drugged and taken against my will.

Footsteps sounded, and I followed the echo to a stairwell across the room. My heart pounded, and I swallowed against a dry throat while my eyes remained fixed on the staircase.

At first, my mind failed to make sense of what I saw, but then I recognized the elaborate costume.

Something flickered at the edge of my vision and I turned to see someone walking up, this man also costumed.

I remembered them now. We hadn't met, certainly hadn't talked, but it was impossible to miss them even in a crowd. They stood out, being not only tall and muscular but wearing impressive costumes that had made me wonder if they were professionals paid to wander the grounds.

Disgust churned my stomach. My initial thought when seeing the pair was how hot they looked. I'd wanted them to talk to me. The demented side of me had wanted to bang them.

They were covered from head to toe in body paint; one in black with pale blue tattoos, the other in ash gray with purple. Both had small twin horns glued to their foreheads and wore long, lithe tails. They were both dressed in all black and matched: open vests and pants in a baggy style tucked into boots. The result was a mash-up of demon meets medieval peasant. They'd undressed, however, and now both approached her, naked and aroused.

"Let me go," I snarled. "Whatever game you think you're playing, you won't get away with it!"

The two men exchanged a glance. One of them, the one painted gray, reached me first and immediately knelt, placing us at eye level. The action caught me off-guard, and I didn't react until he cupped my chin. I screamed into his face, emptying my lungs until I heaved and my throat was burning. He didn't so much as flinch.

"Drink," he commanded, and pressed the lip of a small vial to my mouth.

I shook my head and pursed my lips. He held my face and kept me in place with such ease it terrified me. My frantic head-to-toe struggling barely shook his arm. He pinched my nostrils, and I held my breath, knowing that I would be lucky to last ten seconds at this point.

"There's an easier way," my other kidnapper said in a calm, almost gentle tone.

I fell back as the man holding me instantly released me. When I looked up, it was into a new face. He could have been his friend's twin, and maybe they were, in fact, twins beneath their costumes. Seeing my reflection in his glossy pitch-black contact lenses made me recoil. Naked and afraid. Of all the emotions to be bombarding me, shame was the least welcome and most useless.

"Please." My voice cracked and kept me from going on, but I stared up at him with tears brimming and blurring my vision as I desperately willed my thoughts to come across. Surely he could finish the sentence. Please stop. Please let me go. Please don't do this.

He cupped my cheek, his touch warm and deceiving in its tenderness.

"What is your name?" he asked.

He wiped a tear away with his thumb and I flinched.

My head pounded from the thoughts racing and crashing and tripping over each other to gain the foreground. If there was a reason not to tell him my name, I didn't know it, or maybe I didn't care. I managed to whisper, "Emma."

"I am Vinos," he replied.

I recalled that talking to kidnappers could be a way to guilt them. Sharing personal information was supposed to convince them to go easy on the victim—possibly even let them go. But was that real or just something I'd seen on TV?

"I have a cat," I blurted out. I should have lied and said I had kids, but I was too anxious. "His name is Peanut Brittle, and he has seizures. He needs me."

"What on Earth is she rambling about?" my other kidnapper muttered.

Vinos' gaze flickered to his partner for a moment, but his attention and words were for me. "You will see your cat again. I promise. Drink."

I managed a glare, though I trembled from fear, something he must have noticed. "Let me go. I have a family. Friends. They'll come looking for me."

"They'd never find you here," the other man said.

Vinos smiled an exceedingly patient smile and held up the vial. It was glass and the size of his palm, filled with clear liquid that sloshed as he shook it demonstratively. "This is to keep you safe. A few sips and no harm can befall you."

I didn't believe him and looked away, but he drew my attention back as he tipped the vial to his lips and took a sip.

After he swallowed, he smiled. "See? Not poison. After all, why would we go through the trouble of bringing you here if poisoning you was our intent?"

I'd need a hell of a lot more convincing than that.

Vinos frowned for a moment before taking another sip. Not poison, but it could be a drug to make me compliant. Maybe it wouldn't affect him the same, given that he was twice my size. I glanced at my other kidnapper, unnamed and now a silent observer.

Vinos gripped the nape of my neck, yanking me forward. His lips pressed to mine, and while my hands shoved at his chest, my mouth opened to protest. Mistake.

Sweet, warm liquid poured from his mouth to mine as he kissed me, his lips sealing the liquid from escaping. His tongue coaxed and teased, and in my panic, I swallowed.

The mystery drink tingled going down, a subtle warm prickle that grew as Vinos continued to kiss me, and I, in my stupor, allowed him to. The tingle spread to my fingertips, toes, and everywhere in between. My nipples, already hard from being cold and afraid, puckered painfully now, aching to be touched. But, worst of all, was the warmth and sensitivity blossoming between my thighs. The unmistakable rush of arousal pooled and overflowed, allowing slick moisture to escape.

The drink worked quick—at least, I hoped it was the drink. I hoped I wasn't getting flustered by the kiss. I hoped I had better sense than that.

Vinos traced his tongue around my mouth, and my lips remained parted as I stared up and past him, strangely dazzled by the rainbows hiding within the chandelier's drooping crystals. Glass touched my lips and more liquid came. I drank without fighting it, though I couldn't reason my indifference. The taste and sensation didn't strike me as dangerous—just delicious.

"That's more like it," the other man said. "Now you can see."

The warmth of the mystery liquid settled over me. I almost asked, "see what?" but the scent of lilies and smoke invaded my nostrils and disturbed a slumbering memory. I couldn't reach it, but it was there. Something about the scent.

Vinos kissed me again, a soft press of lips that struck me as innocent and out of place. When he withdrew, I stared at his skin and realized it wasn't painted at all.

My hand twitched at my side and before I could think better of it, I'd reached up and swiped my palm down his cheek and chiseled jaw. I checked my hand for residue. Nothing. But I knew I'd find nothing because his skin was too real. I traced a portion of the swirling blue tattoo that climbed his neck. It was glowing. All of his tattoos were.

"Not a costume," I said. Somehow, saying it aloud made more sense than thinking it. "You're a demon." I looked over at my other captor and saw confirmation in the gentle glow of his violet markings. "Both of you are."

"Yes. Therris and I are both incubi, to be specific," Vinos replied. "You know. The plural of incubus. Demons of lust. Sexual pleasure and desire. I assume you've heard of us through some myth."

"The nectar should be absorbed by now," the now-named Therris said.

Incubus. Right. I knew myself well enough to expect my horrified reaction at any moment now—but it never came. The only thing I felt was... lust. I hungered to be touched. I didn't understand how I could look at Therris' perfect face and still experience such a powerful attraction after finding myself naked and tied to the floor like an animal.

"Whatever you made me drink—is it making me like this? Is it making me want you?"

Vinos appeared amused. "No. The desire and carnal thoughts, along with how you're already aroused—that is all you."

The answer didn't surprise me. I knew the deepest, darkest recesses of my own mind. Vinos had it exactly right. I wanted this.

The mystery. The danger. The submission.

"We'll start your training easy," Vinos said, rising to stand.

I drew into myself, hugging my legs to my chest while the cold floor battled my hot skin. "Training?"

Swinging a small, black paddle idly, Therris joined Vinos in front of me. I kept my gaze high, away from their naked bodies, though it strained my neck to do so. Neither answered me.

83

Therris clicked his tongue and held up the paddle. "You like toys, Vinos."

Vinos rolled his eyes and swiped the paddle from Therris' grip. "Fine. You first."

I suspected I was witnessing a conversation not entirely conducted out loud. Vinos moved to the nearby table and tossed the paddle aside.

Therris caught my attention. I looked up as he crossed his arms.

"On your knees, pet. Show me how you worship."

Chapter 3

Emma

Surreal. What else described kneeling in front of a demon demanding worship of his cock?

The cock in question twitched in impatience, as if it didn't already have my attention. As if I could have ignored the hard ripples of abs and the chiseled vee traced with glowing tattoos angled downward that inevitably drew my attention lower.

It would be a surprise to no one—absolutely no one—that incubi had huge dicks. Not monstrously so, but large enough to put most human men to shame, and larger than I'd ever personally encountered. And because I'd quit trying to fight it—I found myself craving the challenge.

I took his thick shaft in my hand, but my fingers couldn't fully encircle the demon's girth. I didn't have small hands. My hands matched my boyish figure and had often been called "man hands" by the mean girls of my past. At that moment, I felt delicate, and I faced a strong, virile opponent. Fresh desire surged through me as I wrapped my second hand around him and gave a tentative squeeze. He was hot, hard, and one-hundred percent inhuman.

Tattoos swirled around his length, though they didn't glow like the ones on his body. As my hands slid up and down, I realized the markings weren't mere designs on the surface of his shaft. They were raised and firm; intricate ridges that wrapped from the base to the underneath of the flared tip. The strange sensation against my palm filled me with anticipation of having him inside me, his ridges rubbing and stretching my walls.

I glanced up at Therris as my hands slid over him and found him watching me with an unreadable expression. I wanted to please him, and at the moment, he didn't look particularly pleased.

I teased my tongue across the broad head of his cock and licked the bead of arousal that had escaped him. He tasted like spice and flowers, not at all what I expected. I moved to the divot above his taut sac and licked there, then sucked the skin into my mouth. Traveling up, I tasted the length of his silky cock, kissing and nibbling each inch and exploring every enticing, intriguing ridge until I made it back to the top.

The glow of the tattoos low on his hips pulsated, and I took that as a sign that I was doing something right. I licked my lips to wet them before pressing them to the head of his cock, then I slowly took him into my mouth, not stopping until he hit the back of my throat and caused me to wince. He was big. I knew he was big, but I didn't fully comprehend it until it was pushing against my vocal cords and meanwhile, my stacked hands revealed that there was still plenty of him left.

I couldn't imagine doing much more than bobbing on his tip at this point, and that frustrated me. He was a sex demon, and I, a foolish, horny human, wanted to impress him. But I couldn't work a miracle.

I went with it, however, and stroked my hands up and down his shaft as I sucked and licked the part of him that fit in my mouth.

"It won't kill you," Therris murmured.

I licked my lips and peered up at him.

"The nectar you drank protects you."

"What does that mean?"

"Allow me," Vinos said, crossing the room to join us.

A low rumble escaped Therris' throat, and he glared at the other incubus.

Standing behind me, Vinos reached down and framed my face in his hands. His thumbs caressed my cheeks, and he tucked my hair behind my ears.

"Open," he instructed, and after my lips parted, he continued, "like this," and moved me forward to take Therris' cock into my mouth. My gaze went to Therris, but if it bothered him that his partner was essentially aiding in this blowjob, it didn't show.

I bobbed on Therris' length a few times before Vinos scooped my hair into a ponytail, which he wound around his fist until it was sending sharp twinges of pain through my scalp from being pulled too tight. He used my hair as a handle and forced me further onto the hard length. The action took away my control, and my teeth scraped flesh in the process, but it didn't seem to matter.

He pulled my head back just as pressure formed against the back of my throat, and I began to gag. I sucked in air desperately, trying to mentally find my happy place. Emotions scrambled through me, a confusing blend of arousal and panic.

Vinos pushed me forward again, harder and deeper. Involuntary tears stung my eyes, and I tried to back away, but he held me still. He thrust me onto Therris again and again, his grip on my hair painful and exciting at the same time. I couldn't fully comprehend how or why, but his domination over me didn't make me want to fight so much as it made my insides tighten with dark need.

My eyes clenched as I choked. I pounded my fists against

hard thighs, filling my ears with the sound of the clinking chain connecting them, but it made no difference. Vinos gave me a split-second to breathe before he pushed me down again, slowly, patiently, as if I wasn't struggling.

I wanted this, but I couldn't handle it. My nails dug into his muscular thighs and I held my breath for a moment, trying to slow the moment and think. I couldn't think.

My eyes opened, and I looked up through the blur of tears. Therris' glossy black gaze met mine, and a brief wave of calm came over me. I tried to cling to that calmness and took a slow breath. His scent stirred my memories again, but I still couldn't grasp why or what it meant. My jaw ached. My throat was raw. My eyes burned and I could feel spit dripping down my chin.

"Fuck, but I love training a new toy," Vinos growled.

My hair fell around my shoulders, and Vinos retreated, but I only had eyes for Therris. He cupped the back of my head, ready to finish what his friend had started.

He groaned as he forced his way deeper, my throat finally relaxing and opening to him. The sound of his pleasure was like a silky touch along my skin. I wanted to help him. I wanted to feel him when he came for me, and I wanted to taste it, swallow every drop.

He pulled back, his brow creased in concentration or satis-faction, it was hard to tell. I knew he was getting what he wanted from me, and that only made me more eager. His cock was slick with my saliva and he slid it over my bottom lip teasingly before entering my mouth again. I closed my eyes as he pushed into my throat, his hold on my hair keeping me from flinching away.

The feel of him so deep, and the overwhelming awareness of being at his mercy, brought a cloud of dizziness over me. My nose brushed the hard plane of his lower stomach. He'd buried to the hilt, my bottom lip pressing into his sac while saliva dripped to my breasts.

"See, pet?" he drawled. "You give or we take."

Vinos spoke from somewhere behind me. "She enjoys the taking."

I couldn't reply, not that I had anything to say. My face was pressed to Therris' abs, so close that all I saw was a blurry glow against gray demon flesh. He'd held me there for who knew how long, and I was lightheaded. My throat convulsed around him, the discomfort ramping up with each passing second. He released me finally, sending me into a coughing fit.

"Now you know you can handle this," Therris said.

The notion was empowering, not that the glory of being able to deepthroat an incubus lasted long. I didn't have to know everything about the universe to guess that my newly acquired "skill" was thanks to the nectar they'd forced me to consume.

Therris thrust into my mouth, patience gone. He held me by the hair while he fucked my face, and I wanted to purr with pleasure. I savored the feel and spicy taste of him and knew he had to be close.

His climax was like a beacon that called to me. I needed it, and my body was hot and desperate for it, as if it would be my own release.

He hissed and plunged faster. Harder. He was no longer steady, instead chasing down his pleasure with wild strokes.

"Open your mouth," he barked, voice straining. "I want to see my seed on your tongue."

I did as ordered, opening wide as he pulled away and jerked himself off. His arm muscles strained, showing the tension throughout his body. Even his neck was taut, and his jaw was clenched. I watched enraptured as he pumped his fist up and down his cock.

He grunted, and then the first hot stream of his release landed on my tongue. It tingled as I held it there, and he continued to come, each fresh gush landing in my mouth until his cum overflowed and spilled from the corners of my lips.

His chest heaved, and after a moment, a low chuckle escaped him. He stared down at me. "Swallow, pet."

His cum burned down my throat like whiskey, though it tasted spicy and slightly sweet. As I reached up to wipe my lips, my lower belly fluttered and moisture trickled between my legs. I steadied myself against Therris' legs as a sensation crept along my skin, as if an unknown force was intimately caressing me. My pussy throbbed and my nipples ached. He remained still, practically a statue, while I writhed and lost the battle with gravity. I curled up at his feet, my hands slipping between my thighs to sate the sudden need for release.

Waves of pleasure flowed through me, originating from different points on my body. An invisible force nipped at my breasts, ran hands along my sides, and slid teasingly between the wet folds of my drenched pussy.

Vinos appeared and caught my wrists. He held them up, a wicked smile curving his lips. "No touching."

I whimpered. I needed to soothe the ache before it became too much. It didn't make sense, but desperation welled up within me.

Therris swept some of his cum from where it had trailed down my chin and then rubbed his finger across my nipple. I bucked and cried out from the sudden shock of pleasure. It was over-stimulation, I realized, the wild sensitivity that came after I'd climaxed. Everything felt wonderful and yet the sensation was too intense. My body lashed out at the contradiction; wanting more of the offered pleasure but also wanting to kick and scream to escape it.

Chapter 4

Therris

I stroked my cock casually as I watched Emma thrash on the floor, lost to the euphoric after-effect of consuming incubus seed. All humans had a different reaction. Some came. Some cried. Emma made delicious, desperate sounds that made my cock jump against my hand. She was the perfect find.

I knew Vinos would interrupt me. It was in his nature, and after nearly two hundred years of sharing women with him, I'd learned how to trigger him to act. I wanted him to lose his cool and show Emma that beneath his charm, he was just a horny demon who wanted to bend her to his will and slake his lust. She thought too much. I could tell she needed to be shocked.

My gaze roamed her convulsing body. Lean and athletic. Tall, which suited our plans perfectly and made her easier to share. While she begged for release, I searched her thoughts. It was easier to sort through humans' desires when they slept, but lost to her lusty delirium, most of her secrets were out of hiding.

We'd already gleaned much from her, but seeing it again from her perspective helped fuel my drive to wrench every ounce of possible pleasure from our time together. Helping her tap into her darkest desires would keep us sated for weeks. She was exactly the sort of human my kind craved.

I waited until she'd stopped moaning to approach and unfasten her lead from the floor. I gave it a jerk to catch her attention. She hadn't climaxed, despite the torment she'd endured, which thrilled me. The real fun was only just beginning.

Emma shuffled on the ground, eventually crawling to her hands and knees. She was slow to stand, and when she did, her knees shook. The insides of her thighs glistened, and my nostrils flared, taking in the heady scent of her arousal.

Vinos gave me a look. He was a bundle of tension, struggling to hold himself back. I'd seen him like that before, wound tight with hunger. If he snapped completely, he'd go feral and ravish Emma until she was broken and addicted. Which would be great for him, but less fun for me, even if I got to take part.

I needed the self-discovery that humans managed when faced with all we incubi had to offer. Maybe it was delusional, but I liked to think we could sometimes help humans instead of corrupting them.

I wrapped the lead around my fist until the entire length was in my grasp and lifted it into the air, pulling her up against my body by her wrists, until she danced on unbalanced tiptoes so that I could look at her face.

Trails of drying cum showed on the sides of her chin and neck, and the sight made my cock twitch. Vinos would use her throat, too. She would have some time to recover first, but I was already shaking from imagining her choking on his cock while I pounded deep into her cunt.

She stared at me, eyes heavy-lidded. I lowered my hand and shook the lead out, giving her slack. She teetered for a moment before regaining her balance, and the moment she was steady, I walked her around the room. I was looking for the perfect stage for her, and she followed quietly. Her silent obedience fed my desire. Humans were inquisitive, and she was no exception, but for now, she was too dazed to ask questions.

"Onto the horse. Lay down."

She hesitated a moment before sitting on the edge of the furniture I'd indicated, an upgraded style from the simple A-frame bench known as a horse. A glimmer of recognition flashed in her eyes as she looked it over, then her hands gripped behind her for balance, her thumbs indenting the lightly padded vinyl surface. Her eyes met mine, and what she saw made her cease her attempt at prolonging the inevitable. She carefully lay back, frowning as she struggled to find balance.

It was impressive. She'd have had an easier time if she'd instead lain stomach-down on the horse, which had supports on each side and would have put her in a comfortable doggy position. I would have gone along with that position, but I preferred this one; with her body on display, nothing hidden.

The top width of the horse was just shy of the spread of her shoulder blades. She frowned as she fought for balance—which she would have if she'd simply relaxed—and she reached back to hold one end of the horse while allowing her legs to fall open along the sides, her toes skimming the floor.

"You can't be modest," I commented, now realizing why she'd fought relaxing. There was no way for her to lie back and not open her legs wide.

She bit her lower lip and looked away from me. I could read some of her thoughts, but mostly I was tuned to desires and the related emotions, like most incubi. Even with her physical discomfort, she burned with lust.

Vinos moved to stand between her legs. He would take the lead, allowing me to spend more time delving into her fantasies to see everything I could use for our play. He took hold of her hips and swiftly yanked her body toward the end of the horse, eliciting a sharp, astonished cry from Emma. Then he positioned her so that her ass hung off the edge and her parted legs dangled at his sides.

I reached down and grabbed her wrists. Anticipation and a hint of anxiousness glimmered in her brown eyes, and I grinned at her as she fumbled for something to hold.

"You're so wet," Vinos purred to Emma. "I should have known your slutty cunt would be dripping after sucking cock."

A shiver ran through Emma, and I noticed Vinos teasing his fingertips along the insides of her thighs. Her body stretched down the horse in such a way that she had to clamp her thighs around Vinos or be unbalanced. While he distracted her, I secured her cuffs to the end of the bench behind her head, where she'd already instinctively held for stability. When I finished, I reached down to caress her sides, slowly trailing my hands over her waist and rib cage. There were more restraints I could use, but for now, I just wanted her aware of her situation.

Excitement sped her breathing and made it shallow, but her torso gradually relaxed to being stretched out on the horse. Her breasts jiggled lightly with every jagged inhale and exhale. She'd closed her eyes, but her rosy cheeks told me everything I needed to know.

Chapter 5

Emma

I couldn't see Vinos between my legs, but I could sense him. He was close, but not close enough, and not knowing what he planned made my blood race. His touch skimmed the outsides of my thighs and up and around to the insides. The anticipation. The promise of absolute pleasure. It drove me wild.

I didn't understand what had come over me before, but I could make a guess. Incubi would have amazing, magical cum. It made sense. As much sense as waking in a strange place and suddenly discovering that demons existed.

A finger slid along the wet crease of my sex and opened my lips. My back arched to the hot, sudden intrusion. My body wanted to grind against his hand. I craved more. I'd never been so aching with need before, and I'd do anything to slake it.

"I bet you taste delicious," Vinos said.

His low, sultry voice was torture. The words were devastating, and I had to respond. "Please," I whined. "Yes."

"Please what?" he asked, running his finger up and down my slick channel, teasing me but never entering.

I gaped as one by one, my brain cells poofed out of existence.

"Tell us what you want, pet," Therris said.

He'd moved to my side, and I turned my head to see him. He dragged his fingernails lightly around each of my breasts, distracting me for a moment. I wondered if they did that on purpose. Split my attention. I didn't know how to give them equal notice. Did it matter? Did they care?

"I want…" My voice wavered and fell apart. I knew exactly what I wanted. I wanted Vinos to bury his face between my thighs and give me the orgasm that had been looming just out of my reach.

Why was opening my mouth and saying that proving impossible?

Beside me, Therris chuckled. "Self-inflicted torture isn't an intended part of our play. If you can't be honest about your lurid wishes with sex demons, who can you be honest with?"

I exhaled, frustrated with myself because I knew he was right and I knew how ridiculous it was to feel mortified about asking for oral from the demon who'd had me literally choking on his cock mere minutes before. I was naked, restrained, and helpless—and I couldn't make simple words come out of my mouth.

Therris bent down and captured the nipple nearest to him, tugging it between his teeth. The sensation was on the border between mind-blowing and painful, and I wriggled beneath him. My arms were fastened to the end of the bench, limiting how much I could move before I risked sliding off one side of the angled surface. The horse fascinated me, it being one of many things I'd seen in pictures but never experienced.

Being cuffed to one between two incubi was so inconceivable that it could never have appeared on my wildest bucket list. And one of those inconceivable incubi was nibbling my breast.

Somehow, reminding myself of that cleared most of my embarrassment.

"I want you to lick me," I said. In my mind, the statement was firm, but in reality, it was a meek whisper. I stood by it, all the same.

"Good enough," Vinos replied.

Therris straightened. He'd been aggressive at the start, and now he seemed to fade into the background. On purpose. It made me wary and paranoid, but I couldn't remain focused on him when Vinos was moving between my legs.

I had to guess what was happening. He'd knelt, presumably. His breath landed hot against my pussy, and I could sense that he was looking at me. He moved my legs, resting one on his shoulder and wrapping his arm around it to secure my body against his. My eyes clenched in the agony of waiting, and when his tongue slid over the crease inside my thigh, my hips tried to buck, shocked despite the anticipation.

His tongue teased me, each long stroke sparking my blood while he laved my opening and avoided where I desperately wanted him. I couldn't squirm—he held me too tightly. My body's instinct to shift and lift in whatever way possible to achieve the contact I needed was a trapped energy that instead became frantic lust.

"Is it torture?" Therris asked, his voice low and sultry. He'd bent to my ear, and he stroked my cheek gently while his eyes roamed my body.

"Yes," I hissed.

"You know exactly why we picked you, don't you?"

The question sparked something in my mind, but my solid reasoning was impossible to grasp. Therris chuckled and straightened. "Stop tormenting her. It's my turn."

Vinos brushed a sweet kiss to my clit, and then his tongue flicked at the swollen bud, sending wave after wave of sensation

97

through me. I suspected incubus sex could be an addiction, and furthermore, I was likely on my way to being an addict.

Pressure on my temples made my eyes flutter open, and I found Therris staring down at me, his hands holding my face. Images played through my mind. Memories... or no, dreams. Specifically, dreams of sex. Not fantasies, because they weren't images of my making, but they were dreams that I recalled as being arousing.

Reliving the lust-charged moments in quick succession sent me down a wild spiral of pleasure. Vinos' tongue rolled against my clit, inching me ever closer to my looming orgasm. With so many compounding stimulants, I should have reached my peak several times over by now, but something had changed—or rather, they'd done something to me.

The build-up now would bring me to what I knew would be bone-shattering, brain-melting pleasure. I almost feared it, and yet I still chased it down. My skin hummed with the building ecstasy, and I moaned with every press of his tongue to my sensitive bud. My mind danced with the rhythm he set, taking me step-by-step closer to the edge, but just when I thought I had his pattern figured out, he stopped.

I felt unfinished, and then I felt something else entirely. His mouth engulfed my pussy entirely, and he bit down. The edge of his teeth scraped the crest of me, sending a crashing wave of overwhelming rapture through my bones. I screamed as I came, and in the following gasps, as I caught my breath and succumbed to the overlapping crests of my orgasm, I felt a freedom I didn't understand.

I wasn't reserved, or at least, I never thought I was. But I had desires I never dared to express, and a dozen silly sexual hang-ups that I never pondered because they seemed the sort of things that everyone faced. One of those things was that during

sex, I was often quiet. For no reason other than fear of sounding... well, now I didn't even know. I didn't care.

I moaned and whimpered and made every sound that had
previously seemed to be trapped within me until the final throes
of my orgasm had faded into gentle pulses. My body shook
uncontrollably. If I weren't being held, I likely would have fallen to
the floor. It was an experience like no other. Every muscle within
me seemed to spasm. I often had shaky legs after sex, but not
like this.

"Perfect," Vinos purred against my inner thigh.

"And just like that, you're ready for me, dear," Therris said, a
touch of triumph in his voice.

Chapter 6

Emma

My heart pounded in my ears. The rush of blood and the heavy thumping lulled me into a relaxed state —madness, because surely I should have come to my senses and started panicking and seeking escape now.

But no. My greedy self wanted more. Thankfully, more was a given. No chance this encounter ended with oral sex alone. They didn't kidnap me and bring me to—where the fuck were we? I wanted to ask, and maybe if I could form a word I would, but my lips were numb and tingling. My thoughts were fluffy clouds that solidified momentarily and then drifted away.

I quickly returned to my state of longing, forgetting to care about where I was or what existed outside of this dark room.

Firm hands stroked my thighs. Therris nudged my body up until I was centered on the cushioned horse and no longer hanging from one end. He bent my legs and lifted my feet onto the supports at either side, forcing my body to arch before relaxing against the furniture. I had no idea I was this flexible. Another effect of the nectar?

He tightened a strap around my ribs beneath my breasts,

securing me so I no longer worried that I'd topple over if I wiggled too much. I wanted to ask what was next, but all I managed was a deep sigh mixed with pleasure and utter, mindless bliss.

Vinos appeared over me, the light ahead forming a gentle halo around him while his features sank into shadows—an effortless task given his black skin. I blinked and tried to make out his features, but my eyes couldn't separate one dark blur from the next. He stroked my breasts and made a low, feral sound that lifted the small hairs along my skin.

His hands ran from my rib cage to my neck, and he gently pulled me toward him. My body stretched comfortably until my neck arched over the edge of the horse, indicating what he wanted. I swallowed reflexively as my attention settled on his erection, which throbbed with eagerness.

Therris cupped my mound, startling me. I hadn't exactly forgotten him, but clearly, he didn't want to be out of sight and out of mind. Draped over the horse as I was, I couldn't see him, but his presence was a vibrating energy. I didn't need to look down my body to know he stood between my parted legs. I had an image in my mind of him holding his cock and stroking himself as he looked at my wet pussy.

Anticipation gripped me, tightening my body. My nipples ached from the sudden tension running through me. Every inch of me was longing and aware. I could barely contain my desire. My mouth fell open and I puffed a soft breath onto the hard length bobbing just beyond the reach of my lips.

"You want this?" Vinos asked.

His teasing voice dripped with sultry and cocky undertones.

"I want you," I replied huskily.

"What do you want from us?" he asked.

At the other end of my body, Therris positioned the hot,

broad head of his cock along my entrance. I couldn't see him, only feel him, which somehow lent an air of thrill and mystery.

What did I want? "I want everything."

Vinos let out an appraising hmm. "Not as specific as I'd like, but I'm too far gone for patience." He paused for a moment, his hand gripping the base of his shaft tightly. "I can't stretch this out any further for you without losing my mind."

His body and the shadow it cast blocked my vision as he moved the head of his cock to my lips. "Open wide."

I licked my lips and did as instructed, only to gasp as Therris pushed himself into my entrance with one smooth, swift thrust. After being tormented and aroused past the brink of sanity, the sensation of his hardness sinking into me felt like becoming whole. There was a poetic rightness to him pushing into me, his hands gripping my thighs to hold me open to his use.

Vinos slid into my mouth in much the same way. The resistance I'd had earlier was now gone. I wouldn't say it was easy to remain unflinching as his solid length crossed my lips and tongue, but it was familiar.

He pulled back, and I sucked him inch by inch until the head of his cock rested on my tongue weeping arousal and pre-cum. His taste was almost exact to Therris' but with a hint of masculine musk. Inhaling made me dizzy, and I slipped into a dreamy headspace while the sensations from my two lovers warred within.

The experience was pure fantasy brought to life. Were my hands not bound, this would have been a "pinch myself to see if I'm dreaming" moment. With my eyes closed, I was free to drift from second to second, not concentrating but simply feeling.

The horse creaked as Therris moved closer to me. He lifted my hips to meet his slow, deep thrusts. His large size went a touch too deep, hitting the end of me and sending a sharp jolt through me. It was the type of pain that blended into pleasure, and after all I'd endured in the build-up to that moment, I welcomed it with metaphorical open arms.

Vinos followed suit, his hands trailing each side of my neck before clasping in an almost choking manner. He pistoned forward, prodding the back of my throat gently, once, twice, and again. I opened to him, not sure of the exact motion but instinctively knowing that I couldn't lay there unmoving.

They filled me together, moving in and out of my body in perfect synchrony, giving me everything I wanted and needed and was previously too afraid to ask for. My skin prickled with sensitivity as my orgasm built—too soon, I thought. I wanted to stretch the experience and wring out all the ecstasy I could from it before it was over. Therris curled over me, jostling me from my languid mood as he shoved deeper. As he thrust in and out, I somehow grew tighter. It made no sense, as I knew I was slick and ready. He held himself still, buried to the hilt, and my lower stomach fluttered in response to a throbbing sensation that came from where he was hidden within me.

My shock was stifled by the thick cock plunging my throat, coming out only as a garbled vibration of surprise. Each following movement was rougher, both demons moving with a fervor that matched my own growing desperation.

Vinos' hands around my throat tightened, and he pumped into me until the warm skin of his sac jostled against my nose, reminding me of how crude my position was and yet not deterring my need for him. The only problem was that I was finding it hard to remain relaxed for him while the rest of my body tensed at being pounded raw. I was bound and helpless, and the frantic urge to move while restrained only heightened my pleasure.

I was overwhelmed. There was no other way to describe how my thoughts blanked at once. The pleasured grunts and groans cascaded over the dull echo of my rushing blood.

Vinos came first, emptying as Therris had, deep within my

throat and forcing me to hold my breath while his shaft pulsated. My jaw ached, and when he withdrew, I closed my mouth and swallowed, my raw throat coated with him. My tongue was numb, and yet I still tasted him. Spicy and floral.

And then I bucked and screamed, my orgasm taking me by surprise somehow, spurred on by Therris' hand coming down onto my pussy with a harsh slap. He followed up by pinching my clit as he joined his body to mine in a frenzied, racing pace. My scream died, vocal cords exhausted and strained.

Therris had mounted the horse atop me, his throbbing cock stretching me to my limit. I could almost see him, but he was a blur of shadows and glowing streaks. Another climax crested through me as he came and sent a guttural roar echoed through the room, the rawness of it covering me with goosebumps even as the pleasure continued to ebb through my every nerve ending and curl my toes.

He stayed within me, his cock twitching and emptying while I whimpered and caught my breath. I felt shaken to my core, overrun with more than physical bliss. It was almost as if they'd imparted something as they'd come with me, something that lingered and awakened a part of my mind. At the very least, no shame assaulted me as Therris rose and his semi-softened cock slid free, causing a warm spill of liquid between my thighs.

Then he did the unexpected, as his fingers scooped his spilling seed and pushed it back into my sore channel. My eyes rolled back, and I moaned his name.

Chapter 7

Therris

Too much pleasure had taken its toll, rendering Emma a limp heap of flesh and bone that I was more than happy to clean up and carry to bed.

The dungeon façade was gone, replaced with a replica of Emma's bedroom as taken directly from her unconscious. A tiny tug of disappointment had gone through me at erasing the dark interior and bondage furniture. She'd never asked where she was, and I'd wanted to tell her.

Though in reality, we'd brought her to our home world—Pandəmonium—the room she'd seen existed on Earth and was part of her past. She'd never seen the room in person, but her memories held a single, longing moment of staring at the arched stairwell that led to that dungeon, a place she hadn't mustered the courage to enter before.

I suspected if the opportunity presented itself again, she would have no trouble descending the stairs.

Vinos stood at my shoulder, watching her slumber as I did.

"It's always a shame that they can't remember," he murmured.

I nodded my agreement and didn't add my lamentation. Our encounter could awaken at random through a dream when her unconscious was flipping through memories, but it would never be something that stuck with her once her eyes were open. At best, it could spark a moment of déjà vu.

"Cassian touched her," I mentioned instead.

"I saw. She was at his club. I didn't see a memory of the meeting, however."

"He just slipped into her dream. Probably for the same reason we found ourselves lured to her."

"I don't understand why he stopped."

Vinos spoke with a scoff, but we both knew why Cassian had stopped visiting Emma's dreams. As the owner of a sex club, he never ran short on dreams to feed through, and unlike most incubi, he was content with dreams and sex in human form. He never made use of the pocket dimension where we'd brought Emma, a sliver of Pandemonium accessible only to incubi, succubi, and the humans they entertained.

"Cassian's a fool," I muttered, a bit too loudly.

Emma stared at me, having awakened within the last few seconds.

"Who is Cassian?" she asked sleepily.

"The incubus who had been fucking you in your dreams. Though, it seems to have been a few years since he touched you," I replied simply. "But as you've witnessed, there's a cap to pleasure in dreams. Here, everything is heightened."

"And here is..." her voice drifted off, and she stared down at herself, no doubt recognizing the teal comforter of her bed. "This isn't real."

"You're still in our playroom," Vinos said. "The slice of existence where we bring human toys to torment or pleasure—or both—to our hearts' content."

The corner of her mouth tugged upward into a mischievous grin. "I see. Since I'm still here, does that mean we aren't done?"

I exchanged a glance with Vinos. We were, by our very nature, insatiable, and could wear a human out if we weren't careful. Still, I wanted another embrace with Emma before we had to say goodbye.

Vinos tilted his head, answering the unspoken question. He then joined Emma on the bed, pulling her from her resting position to sprawl across his lap.

She giggled, the sound husky with lust. They kissed hungrily before Emma pushed him away to look at me.

"I'll never see you again after this, will I?" she guessed.

"Hard to say," I admitted. "You wouldn't recognize us, but you may see us."

Her brow scrunched. "Meaning?"

"For reasons too lengthy to explain, we can't enter your dreams in the future. But perhaps we'll run into each other," I said.

"What he means is as humans. We have human bodies, and we enjoy using them. Obviously, dreams are delightful and are what we're known for, but flesh against flesh is transcendence. Particularly here, where we have the power to grant your every fantasy," Vinos said while palming her breast and staring into her eyes.

"Oh," she said breathily, half in understanding and half in pleasure.

Vinos freed her from the comforter swathed haphazardly around her body and rocked her naked body against his erection. "Enough talk."

"Yes," she hissed, as he bent down to suck on her breast.

Her arched body sent blood rushing through me and left me lightheaded—me, an incubus! The woman was poetry and

109

passion come alive. I climbed onto the bed and knelt behind her, sandwiching her between Vinos and my body.

"Yes," she moaned again, this time in response to my fist in her hair as I stretched her head to one side and bit down on her neck.

"Ride him," I urged.

She lifted her body, her hips undulating between us. When she sank down, Vinos exhaled and visibly pulsed with desire, his tattoos momentarily brighter than before. He held her waist and thrust upward into her, matching her slow rhythm. I cupped her breasts and kissed her neck as I tasted the electric pleasure trickling through her body, drawing it into myself in small pulls to avoid being greedy.

Her skin was hot and salty with sweat. I licked and sucked her neck until the flesh turned pink and red, wanting to leave my mark on her, absurd as it was. She was just another human, one of many. Except somehow, she wasn't.

Sweet sounds of bliss escaped her throat, vibrations beneath my mouth. I shifted behind her and ground my hard length against the soft mounds of her ass.

"Let me in," I half-growled.

"Not there," she gasped and shook her head so quickly I nearly laughed.

She had no idea what she'd just invited. I squeezed her lovely breasts before trailing down the sides of her lithe torso and cupping her bottom. I slid my hand between our bodies and beyond until I found the taut opening of her body stretched around Vinos. I teased my finger along her cunt until the tip slipped in and joined Vinos' thrusting cock.

"Oh," she moaned. "Oh fuck…"

"If I can't go there, I'll go here," I said into the soft shell of her ear. "What do you say to that?"

"You-you won't fit," she rasped.

"I'll make it fit," I promised, the very thought sending a primal surge through my bones.

Vinos lay back on the bed, pulling her forward with him to give me a better angle to join in. Emma simply whimpered. She didn't need to speak, however. We all knew she wanted everything the two of us could give her, and she thrived under our domination.

I used Emma's arousal to wet my cock before pressing it beside Vinos'. As long as the nectar continued to flow through her, she could take this, though it wouldn't be easy. Her heart pounded, and her breathing was ragged and anxious. I felt her fear but recognized it for the shallow layer it was, barely coating the tumult of raging, dark need beneath.

Vinos exited her completely, and I took both our cocks in hand to guide them into Emma's ready cunt. It was a slow thrust, and she shook and squeaked from the effort. Her walls squeezed violently against us, the vise-like grip nearly enough to send me over the edge immediately. I massaged her breast as I slid within her, gradually gaining depth.

We alternated our thrusts with hard-fought patience while Emma bit her lip and rocked her hips in an effort to find comfort.

"Breathe," I whispered.

She pouted a little, and I imagined that were her eyes open instead of clenched tight, they would have rolled at my words.

"You're doing so well, pet," I said, using the task of reassuring her to distract from my body's urge to force my way deeper without a care for her pain. "How does it feel to be stretched around two demon cocks?"

Red blossomed on her cheeks instantly. "I-it hu-hurts," she hissed. "But s-so good."

Her words trailed into a long sigh.

Vinos' hips lifted, jostling us all and alerting us to the fact that he'd bottomed out. I thrust deep and buried myself full as well. My hold on Emma tightened, and I twisted one hard nipple between my fingers as our pace sped. I couldn't see the depths of my wanting for her, I only knew that my body demanded more from her. More of her moans. More of her trembling. More of her sweet walls shuddering in release around my cock.

She writhed between us as we groped her, touching her everywhere, kissing her wherever we could reach. Pleasure looped through us like a never-ending circuit, multiplying as we went on.

"Fuck," she cried.

Her orgasm lingered just out of reach. I sensed it, and I knew Vinos felt it as well. We could force it to hover there and build, and as I thought of it, Vinos' magic trickled through her to make it happen.

"Yes," I agreed. "Fuck. We're fucking you how you need to be fucked, aren't we?"

She didn't answer, only lulled her head back as her body shook between us. Her breathing staggered and matched us as we moved; in and out, her walls tightening against our cocks as if to hold us deep and still. Magic accompanied every hard stroke; I couldn't help it. She was already full and tight, her body already stretched and giving us pleasure, but the rampant wish to give her more, to give her everything, won over.

My cock swelled within her, pressing her walls until she was shaking and muttering nonsense. Vinos dug into her hips and held her down, grinding our straining cocks against her cervix and locking her in place. I wrapped a hand around her throat, and she instinctively sucked in a deep breath before I squeezed her windpipe.

Closing my eyes, I leaned into her hair and breathed in her sweet scent while I listened to her racing pulse. She grabbed my arm, her fingernails sinking into me. She twitched once. Twice. I released her neck as Vinos freed her orgasm, and she came in an explosion of shuddering and full, throaty screams.

The energy that flowed from her climax brought Vinos and me over the brink with her, and together we spent our loads deep into her quivering channel.

Epilogue

mma

Six months later

I never thought I'd set foot in Ephemeral again. I'd come seven years ago when I was in my early twenties and thought I was ready for adventure. I hadn't been.

Ephemeral was, simply put, a sex club. A rather well-known one to anyone familiar with such places.

Stepping through the outer entrance after paying and signing a behavior waiver, I entered the welcome room. Memories assailed me of what awaited beyond the multiple doorways covered with color-coded velvet curtains.

My attention landed upon the large mural painted on the main wall. The artist—the owner of the club—had been inspired by the classic painting, "Hylas and the Nymphs," which portrayed the image of a young man being lured into the water by a group of naked women; water nymphs. The original was sensual but innocent. The recreation on the walls was provocative. No dark water or bodies hidden by lily pads.

Two nymphs with large breasts stroked the man's straining cock while the other ladies watched and touched themselves or each other. I found myself drawn to it now as I had been that long ago night. It symbolized the club's ambiance perfectly. Ephemeral was a place of passion and beauty. Even in their dark rooms, there was no seedy feel. Sex wasn't crass, but an adventure meant to be explored.

"This turns you on," a voice said. "The air hums with your ardor."

I glanced toward the speaker, recognition coming instantly. "Cassian."

"You remember," he cooed.

I nodded. He'd given me a quick tour all those years ago. Somehow, he looked exactly the same. "I guess that means you remember me, too."

"I never forget a pretty face."

I smiled, though I recognized it for the line it was. He was handsome and charming, and even though when he spoke his eyes held devoted attention, I didn't fall for it. He owned this place. He undoubtedly participated in orgies non-stop and thought of all women as pretty faces.

A glass of champagne appeared in his hand and he extended it to me. "I won't keep you," he said and gestured around the room. "Please. Enjoy."

Enjoyment was already on my mind, and I took the glass with a nod. The last six months of my life had been leading to my return to Ephemeral, ever since I woke up from a mysterious mead-induced nap at the Renaissance festival. I'd had an awakening I didn't understand, but I blamed it on the very sexy pirates who did a raunchy comedy show before the final curtain.

Regardless, here I was, and I knew exactly what I wanted.

To my left was a dusky rose curtain, to my right, one of deep violet. I sipped my champagne and went through the doorway to the right and kept straight down the paneled white corridor and into an open space broken up by tall dividers. I ignored the whispers, moans, and the wet slap of flesh against flesh, knowing that if I looked up I'd see couples writhing on every flat surface. I continued into a corridor that ended at an ornate, carved archway over a winding staircase.

My stomach flipped in nervous anticipation. My skin hummed with excitement and yet I remembered that I'd failed to take these steps once before. I swirled my drink, watching the steady stream of bubbles dancing to the surface, and then I downed it in one inelegant gulp. I set the glass down on a nearby table and headed down the stairs.

The walls and steps darkened in color as I descended, and by the time I reached the landing, everything was black. Black paneled walls. Black tile floor. Black furniture. Crystal chandeliers hung overhead, but their sophistication couldn't change what the room was. A dungeon.

A flutter of arousal tightened my core, followed by a brief flicker of déjà vu as if I'd wondered and fantasized about this moment for so long that I thought I'd already experienced it. I'd wanted to be in this room seven years ago. Instead, my desires and cravings had terrified me and after wandering in circles upstairs, I'd hidden in a corner for an hour before returning to my hotel room and drinking wine until I passed out.

But that was old Emma. New Emma was going to do more than watch.

My attention wandered to a naked man stretched out on a vinyl-topped table situated below hanging chains. Another man was cuffing a woman onto the chains so that she'd be straddling the naked man. The scene sent heat through my blood.

Bodies moved around me, and I moved away from the stairs

117

to not be in the way. Two men flanked me where I chose to stand and observe.

"Do you like that?" one asked.

I glanced over both men, both tall with chiseled features. One with blue-black hair that fell to the collar of his black buttoned shirt, the other with blond hair cut in a shortish preppy style I liked to call "the frat boy."

Either of them could be fun tonight if they didn't turn out to be creeps. I shrugged at the question. "I'm not sure what I'd like tonight."

The blonde flattened a hand against the small of my back and gently angled me to one side of the room. He hadn't asked to touch me, but before I could protest, I saw what he meant to show me.

"What about that?" he asked, his voice a low rumble.

Goosebumps tickled me from head to toe as I watched a vibrator sliding slowly into a woman strapped down to a padded horse.

"We could have fun together," his friend said and leaned down to nibble my neck.

Memories sparked, but nothing solid. Just blurred dreams and an undeniable wave of desire I couldn't explain. The man kissing my neck tilted my face to his and licked my bottom lip.

"Let us give you what you want, pet," he said.

I stared into his dark eyes as he pulled me close. The scent of flowers and smoke filled my nostrils and tugged at my insides. Something about him was familiar but more reminiscent of a fantasy than any reality I'd ever known.

His friend closed in on me from behind, and their hard bodies pressed against me stoked the simmering fires of my lust.

"Yes," I replied. "I just decided what I want."

About the Author

Godiva Glenn is a nocturnal being, much like vampires and cats. She specializes in weaving paranormal romance fiction that transports readers into enchanting worlds where love and the supernatural collide. Her catalog spans shifters, fae, demons, and more.

She grew up surrounded by books thanks to her grandfather, an avid reader himself. Through weekly trips to the library, she devoured books, from adventures in babysitting to worlds of magical knights and powerful queens. However, it wasn't until she read her first romance novel in her early twenties that her creative spirit caught fire. She realized that she absolutely needed to give life to her own characters and worlds, and she embarked on a journey to become an author.

Godiva lives in the U.S. with dreams of traveling abroad to research locations in person.

Also, she does not bite and is relatively pleasant to socialize with.

Facebook * Twitter * Goodreads * Bookbub

For updates, sneak peeks, and exclusive content, join Godiva's mailer: www.godivaglenn.com/sign-up/

Also by Godiva Glenn

~NIGHT WOLVES~

Night Revelations

Night Born

Night Surrender

Night Caught

Night Forgiven

Night Stolen

∼

Visit GodivaGlenn.com for the full catalogue!

Made in the USA
Columbia, SC
04 July 2025

60096401R00076